"A couple," Bill said, his voice heavy with awe

"Right. Like a disguise. We'd be a disguise for one another. My people won't be looking for a couple, either," Cara reasoned.

Bill shook his head, trying to clear it. "Wait a minute," he said. "Less than an hour ago you thought I was a murderer and, in fact, I did attack you and tie you up. Why should you trust me now?"

And for that matter, why should I trust you? Bill thought.

"Or why should you trust me?" Cara added.

"Are you a mind reader, too?"

Cara shrugged and shot him a complacent grin. "Isn't the enemy you know safer than the one you don't know?"

Dear Reader,

Be prepared to meet another "Woman of Mystery"!

We're proud to bring you another book in our onging WOMAN OF MYSTERY program, designed to bring you the debut books of writers new to Harlequin Intrigue.

Meet Molly Rice:

For Molly there was never any doubt she'd become a writer; at the age of four she began a lifelong obsession with notebooks and pencils, which only recently transferred itself to an obsession with computers. Somewhere in between, she discovered the excitement of the public library and the rest, as they say, is history. Molly lives in St. Paul, Minnesota, with her husband, but has threatened to run away to Santa Cruz ever since she spent a month there developing the inspiration for this book.

We're dedicated to bringing you the best new authors, the freshest new voices. So be on the lookout for more "Woman of Mystery" books!

Sincerely,

Debra Matteucci
Senior Editor & Editorial Coordinator
Harlequin Books
300 East 42nd Street
New York, NY 10017

Silent Masquerade
Molly Rice

Harlequin Books

TORONTO • NEW YORK • LONDON
AMSTERDAM • PARIS • SYDNEY • HAMBURG
STOCKHOLM • ATHENS • TOKYO • MILAN
MADRID • WARSAW • BUDAPEST • AUCKLAND

This book is dedicated to the Schuck family who have been my own and only family for so many years: Charles, Velma, James, Patricia, Faye Simpson, Edward, Juanita and Stan Harris, Dorothy and Ted McDonald, and Elizabeth.
To Elizabeth Harri, who waits for my books
with flattering impatience.
And most special thanks to Virginia Beasley Jackson,
my friend and sister forever.

ISBN 0-373-22315-3

SILENT MASQUERADE

Copyright © 1995 by Marilyn Schuck

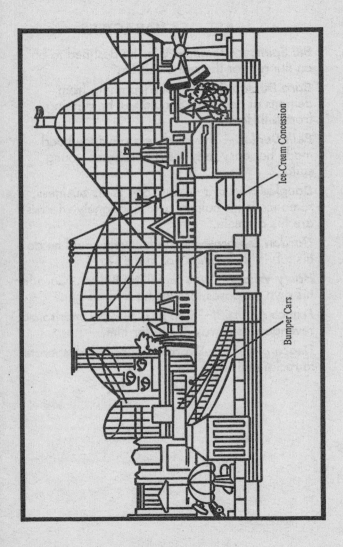

Ice-Cream Concession

Bumper Cars

CAST OF CHARACTERS

Bill Spencer/Hamlin—Was he destined to be on the run for the rest of his life?

Cara Dunlap/Davis—She's running from demons of her own. Should she be running from Bill Hamlin?

Beth Dunlap—The loneliness of widowhood made her easy prey for a handsome young suitor.

Douglas Harvard—Marriage is his business, romance is his calling card and lonely widows are his clientele.

Gordon Lefebre—How effectively could he do his job if his feelings got in the way?

Harry Wilder—Was he tailing Bill and Cara for his own purposes, or was he a hired gun?

Franco Alvaretti—Mob boss recently imprisoned; revenge was a way of life for him.

Deacon Avery—Alvaretti's attorney; desperate to reclaim his own life.

Chapter One

Bill Spencer had known for some time that he wasn't going to trust his life to the protection of any government agency. He was too familiar with the mechanics of the bureaucratic system to put his faith—his life—in their hands. He knew there were moles in high places, leaks in the system's plumbing.

But he needed to use the agency to front his escape.

He needed the Organization to think he'd gone into the Witness Protection Program, so they'd be off sniffing in that direction while he made his getaway to parts unknown, covering his tracks with the expertise he'd acquired while working both sides of the fence.

For that reason, there were two sets of papers in his pocket, one given to him by the WPP, the other a set he'd spent many nights crafting himself, not even trusting one of the specialists whose markers he held.

If he'd learned nothing else during the two years he worked with a foot in both camps, he'd learned that there was always the possibility of betrayal when you were dealing with other human beings.

He made another sweep of the room. The least little clue could be magnified by the right intelligence team and used to begin the tracking that would lead them to him.

He was just running his hand between the mattress and the box spring when the knock came at the door.

"We're ready to go, Spencer," a male voice said softly.

He looked around the room and nodded, satisfied that it was clean, then picked up his bag and his briefcase. He was ready.

They led him out of the hotel, a man on either side of him, two in the rear, one scouting a few feet in front.

He got into the rear of the limo, again flanked by two of the agents, and did his own survey of the street as the chauffeur looked right and left before pulling out of the drive. There was no sign of anyone from the Organization

No sighting didn't mean that nobody was out there, it just meant they couldn't be seen. Keeping his paranoia in place had saved his behind more than once, and he wasn't about to give it up now. But the fact was, it worked in his favor if they had a man watching him now, someone who'd report back that he'd gone off with the WPP agents. The red herring.

At the airport, he picked up the ticket the agency had reserved in the name Stanley Springer, checked his bag through to Madison and moved purposefully toward the blue concourse. The five men circled him, keeping a watchful distance, but staying close enough to move in if he was targeted.

He nodded distantly at the agent near the water fountain and went into the men's room. The cubicles were all empty. He chose the one farthest from the door, locked himself inside and opened the briefcase.

When he left the men's room, he nodded again, but this time there was no recognition in the agent's eyes. The agent was merely responding politely to a stranger's passing nod.

He went to the Western Airline counter, picked up a ticket in the name of Sam Spalding, checked the briefcase through to San Francisco, and then left the terminal through the sliding glass doors.

The car, stashed in long-term parking, was covered with dust. He drove to a self-serve car wash and hosed it down. Then, making sure there was nobody lurking around to observe his actions, he got a tool kit out of the trunk and removed the plates, replacing them with another set he'd lifted from a junkyard and kept for just such a purpose.

There was a suitcase in the trunk, as well. He slipped out of the coveralls he'd donned in the men's room at the airport, took off his suit coat and tie and put on a cardigan sweater from the bag. Last he threw the blond wig, fake mustache, baseball hat and horn-rimmed glasses he'd been wearing into the trunk and slammed it shut.

He was back on the highway seven minutes after he'd pulled into the car wash.

It took him five days to get to his destination, five days in which he barely slept, ate only fast food picked up at drive-through windows and made countless out-of-the-way detours to obscure his route. Outside a small town called Widow's Peak, located at the top of a hill that looked out over the Atlantic Ocean, he put the car in drive and gave it a shove, watching as it rolled down the hill facing away from the town. The car careened into the gorge below and then, after only a moment, exploded. He waited until he was sure the fire had consumed all but the steel chassis, now charred almost beyond recognition, tossed a duffel bag over his shoulder and proceeded on foot into town, where he caught the Greyhound bus that was just boarding passengers on their way back to the Midwest.

CARA DUNLAP put the car in gear and rolled out of the driveway without starting the engine. When the car rolled onto the asphalt road, she started the engine and turned in the direction of the highway. Forty minutes to Boston, she figured, and then she'd leave the car and find other transportation. Boston might be a good city to get lost in, but it was too close to home. No, if she was going to do this, she was going to have to do it right. And that meant getting as far from Greensville as possible, and as quickly as possible. Once she got to Boston, she'd have to decide where to go from there.

By morning they'd have discovered she was gone, and found her note. She prayed her mother would let her go, wouldn't try to find her. But her only hope for avoiding discovery, just in case, was a good head start—and not knowing where she was going herself.

In Boston she left the car on a side street, hailed a cab to the Greyhound station and bought a ticket for the next bus leaving the terminal.

She caught the bus just as the driver had loaded the last passenger and was locking the baggage compartment at the side of the bus.

"No luggage, miss?" he asked.

"Uh-uh," she said, out of breath from running through the terminal. "Just this." She held up a gym bag that contained a couple changes of clothing and a few personal items. The bag would fit under her seat or in an overhead compartment.

"Okay. We're all set to roll, then."

There were no single vacant seats. Cara sat down next to a man who wore a slouch hat pulled low over his eyes and appeared to be sleeping. She took a couple of deep, calming breaths before closing her own eyes in sheer exhaustion.

San Francisco, a big city, and one far enough away. About as far as you could get from Greensville, Massachusetts, without leaving the country. She'd have to find a job, a place to stay. Could she do that without identification?

She didn't think she'd need to prove her identity to a landlord, but sooner or later an employer would ask for a social security number.

She wriggled in her seat, uneasily aware that she might have done better to plan ahead, lay some groundwork, before taking off. But then she would have been at greater risk of discovery. She'd watched enough TV, read enough books, to know that too much planning was usually what got people caught. Spur-of-the-moment was best. She had enough cash in her bag to buy a small working wardrobe, pay a couple of month's rent and keep herself in bologna sandwiches and soft drinks until she had a job.

The man beside her snored softly and then made a little whimpering sound as he twisted slightly in his seat. She opened her eyes and gave him a sideways glance. His hat had fallen forward even more, and his head was now tilted in her direction. She wondered if she should take his hat before it fell off completely. But then she might risk waking him.

She eased over a little, hoping he'd slipped as far to her side as he was going to. She shut her eyes again, willing sleep to give her a few hours without the stress of her thoughts.

She was in a light doze when her neighbor's head fell with a soft thud against her shoulder. Instantly awake, she craned her head to look down at him without moving her body.

Just as she'd thought, his hat had fallen off, rolling from his lap to the floor. Without it she could see, in the dim light cast from the low-wattage overhead bulb, that he had thick dark hair, a short beard, long black lashes that swept high cheekbones and a soft-looking full mouth that made him appear vulnerable in sleep.

In the small, enclosed space, she detected a hint of aftershave or hair cream, a popular masculine fragrance that had a clean, sharp tang to it. He gave another soft snore, and she noticed that his breath was warm and sweet.

There was comfort in his solid weight, in the feel of his curls just touching her neck; she could pretend that she was not alone, friendless, cast homeless into an unknown future. If he awakened while lying on her shoulder, she could always pretend she had been asleep and wasn't aware he'd slumped against her.

She closed her eyes, and in moments she, too, was sleeping.

THEY AWAKENED simultaneously. Sunlight streamed in through the bus windows, making Cara blink in astonishment.

The man next to her sat up and frowned. "Sorry," he muttered. "I have a tendency to do that on buses." He felt around and then leaned forward to rescue his hat.

"S'okay," Cara mumbled, looking away in embarrassment now that broad daylight exposed them so ruthlessly to one another.

He was terribly handsome, with dark blue eyes and a short growth of beard, and he was older, she realized, than he'd appeared while sleeping. But something about him seemed out of sync. It dawned on her that he didn't seem the type to ride the bus. For some reason, he struck her as more of an executive type than a working stiff, despite his blue jeans and brown leather jacket.

She glanced down at his hands, which were busily trying to reshape the felt hat, and saw that they were long and well shaped, with blunt, clean fingernails. If he's a blue-collar worker, he does his work with gloves on, she thought.

Cara peered past him to the scenery beyond the window. Farmland. But there were a lot of billboards whizzing by, an indication that they were nearing a town. She wondered what time it was, how far they were from their final destination.

Her neighbor started to rise. "Excuse me," he said. "I need to stretch my legs."

Cara stood up to let him into the aisle. She could see from his height that his legs must indeed have been cramped. She was tall for a woman, five foot eight, and he was about six inches taller.

He went back to the rest room, and she smiled to herself, thinking he'd used the euphemism to spare her embarrassment. She leaned across his seat to see out the window better, and his scent assailed her senses once again. She saw a sign that boasted a full-service rest stop and felt the bus slow down as it prepared to turn onto a wide blacktop drive.

Her seatmate returned just as she was rising to join the other passengers for the rest stop. "I guess we're stopping for breakfast," she said.

"Looks that way." He stood back to let her get out and precede him off the bus.

In the restaurant, Cara went straight to the ladies' room, thankful to find there wasn't a long line in front of the cubicles. She washed up as best she could with the public amenities and ran a small purse-size brush through her red-gold hair. Her curls had begun to tangle from sleeping on the bus, and it took her a few minutes to get the brush through the mess. She retucked her white linen blouse into her khaki skirt and straightened her collar.

When she returned to the café area, she saw her bus-mate sitting alone in a booth near the windows with a plate of food already in front of him. On impulse, she decided to join him.

"Do you mind if I sit with you?" she asked, standing beside the booth.

He gestured to the other bench. "I guess it's the least I can do, after using your shoulder for a pillow all night."

He barely glanced at Cara as she ordered coffee and toast from the waitress, but when they were alone, he said, "I don't remember you being on the bus when I fell asleep."

She shook her head, smiling. "You were asleep when I got on in Boston."

He nodded and resumed eating.

"You must have been on the bus quite a while before I got on," Cara said, making polite small talk.

"Why? What do you mean?" the man demanded.

Cara blinked in surprise. There hadn't been anything offensive in her remark.

"Oh, look," the man said, running his hand across his jaw. "I'm sorry I snapped liked that. Sleeping sitting up always makes me a little cranky."

"That's all right," Cara said, "I was just making friendly conversation." As if to confirm that, she added, "As long as we're seatmates, we may as well introduce ourselves. I'm Cara D—Davis."

"Bill Hamlin." The new name came easily its first time on his lips, but he hadn't missed the girl's hesitation over her own last name. Now what could that be all about?

She seemed too old to be a runaway, and yet he had a gut feeling that she was on the run. Maybe it takes one to know one, he thought, or maybe it's a case of thinking everyone's tarred with the same brush you are.

"Going to San Francisco?"

Bill nodded. "I guess."

"You guess?" She put her cup back in its saucer and stared at him. "Don't you know?"

He recovered quickly. "You thought I said 'guess'? I said 'yes.'"

She nodded, but there was a skeptical gleam in her eyes.

Bill mopped up the last of the yolk on his plate with a piece of biscuit and popped it in his mouth. A whole week of fast food had made him greedy for the taste of something real. It was almost worth the long, uncomfortable bus ride to have a chance to eat something a little closer to homemade at the various stops along the route.

Sated at last, he took a final swig of coffee and then concentrated on the girl, whose attention was now absorbed by her own meager breakfast.

Her hair was a blaze of colorful curls, and he remembered that when he awakened, his first sense had been that he smelled something wonderful. He realized now that it had been her hair. Every time she moved her head, the light, spicy scent wafted toward him. Her hair was her most arresting feature. Her eyes were brown, and she had a dusting of freckles across her nose and cheeks that precluded any chance of her ever being considered glamorous. But her smile revealed fine, even white teeth and a dimple in her right cheek. In a flash of insight, he realized that she was the kind of woman who would become really beautiful in the close-up lens of a camera, or in the eyes of someone who saw her day after day.

She ate slowly, breaking the toast in bite-size pieces with her fingers. He found himself mesmerized by the ritual. When she looked up and saw that he was watching her, a slight blush rose to her cheeks and her eyes lit with humor.

"Have I got butter on my chin?" she asked, smiling.

"I've never seen anyone eat toast like that," he answered.

She laughed. "It lasts longer this way, and makes less of a mess."

He wondered why she wanted to make it last, but didn't ask.

When she looked at her check, he saw that she counted out the exact amount of her bill from a little change purse that she held close to her chest.

So, she had limited funds and she was on the run.

Ordinarily, he would have been intrigued by the mystery; it was, after all, his life's work to solve the puzzles of human behavior. But he was through with all that now and didn't dare risk any kind of involvement with strangers that might eventually lead his enemies to him.

No, not enemies. Enemy. Just one. One man in the whole world who had the power, even from behind the locked bars of a maximum-security prison, to snuff out his life. As long as Franco Alvaretti was alive, "Bill Hamlin" would be forced to live the half life of those who went underground.

It was war. And the whole world was mined with explosives. One wrong step, and it was all over.

Automatically he raised his hand to feel his beard, reassured when he felt its soft downiness. A couple more days and the beard would be as full and natural-looking as if he'd had one for years.

As they left the café to reboard the bus, Bill took sunglasses from his jacket pocket and put them on.

When he offered her the window seat, telling her he'd had enough of rolling scenery, Cara took the inside seat and thanked him.

Bill read for a while, forcing himself to concentrate on the pages of a book written by an agent he'd once worked with in the Middle East. The joke in the Service was that old agents didn't die, they went to press. The book was good, unfolding an espionage tale that might well have been taken from the very records Bill himself had once helped compile.

He kept his place in the book with his finger and closed his eyes, his mind drifting back of its own accord.

"We need you back home, Spence. There's an opening in Alvaretti's organization, and if you move fast and with the right credentials, we can do what we've always wanted—get a man inside to overturn Alvaretti's operation."

He'd had the right credentials. Alvaretti had taken him on after only a couple of days of consideration, and he'd became privy to the legitimate books in Alvaretti's accounting department—but not the books that the FBI, the CIA and the IRS were panting to uncover. That had taken time. He'd had to find a way to get into the man's good graces before he was trusted with the other side of Alvaretti, Inc.

It had taken eighteen months. During that time he'd been tried by fire more than he cared to remember, once by being forced to stand by with his mouth shut while members of Alvaretti's goon squad worked a man over until he was nearly dead.

When he was finally allowed into the inner sanctum of the organization's workings, he'd thought it was merely a matter of photocopying the evidence and getting out. He had never anticipated the end result—that the agency would have to bury him, that from that moment on, Alvaretti wouldn't rest until he got his revenge.

His superiors had talked about plastic surgery, a faked death, the Witness Protection Program. The WPP seemed the least drastic, in Spence's mind, and he had determined then not to relinquish control of his life to anyone else. He knew now that the government had deliberately used him in its frenzy to get Alvaretti, and that once he'd done the job he was no longer of any use to them.

I should have realized up front that there was no other way out once I went in, he told himself for the umpteenth time. He ground his teeth and clenched his fists. The worst of it was that he really missed his job; it was work he'd known he wanted to do since he'd been a schoolboy. There was pain in recognizing how much he'd lost. He took a deep breath to push away the ache.

Cara felt movement beside her and drew her attention from the passing scenery to glance sideways at Bill. "Are you all right?" she whispered, seeing the devastation on his face, his rigid body language.

He blinked, forced himself to relax and nodded, a tiny line of sweat beading his forehead. "Yeah. Fine. Don't worry."

Cara wasn't so sure. He looked sick, as if he were about to have a seizure or something, or as if he were experiencing incredible pain. "I've got some aspirin in my purse," she said softly. "Would that help?"

He shook his head and then leaned back against the headrest. "No, thanks. I think I just need to sleep for a while." He closed his eyes.

Cara turned back to the window but couldn't get this last image of him out of her mind. It brought to mind news clips of the hostages just released from years of incarceration in the Middle East. But he was none of her business, after all. She'd offered her help, and she'd been refused. She had enough troubles of her own without adding his to her list.

Nevertheless, when they pulled into a bus station for their lunch stop, she suggested they eat their meal together.

He looked hesitant at first, but then shrugged, as if to say "What harm can it do?" For some reason, Cara found that gesture strangely disturbing. It made her feel insignificant; though they were only strangers passing a day and a night together by accident, she felt as if she would have liked to make a better impression on him.

Bill told himself that this interlude for the brief time they were travelers together couldn't lead to anything dangerous. The girl was good company. She didn't chatter away, as some travelers did, and yet she was friendly and open.

Well, not entirely open. There was that business about her name. And he'd noticed that whenever they came to a town, she put her hand up along the side of her face that was nearest the window, as if she were afraid someone in one of those towns would recognize her.

In the station coffee shop, Cara ordered a small dinner salad and iced tea, while Bill took the waitress's recommendation of the blue plate special.

"How do you keep your figure, eating like that?" Bill asked, gesturing toward Cara's tiny bowl of salad.

"This *is* how I keep my figure," Cara said with a grin.

But when she ordered the same thing at the supper stop, Bill thought again that Cara must be short on funds and unable to afford a complete meal. It made him nervous to eat with her, and he couldn't help but worry about her health. Wouldn't she get sick if she didn't get some real food into her?

He told himself that his only reason for being concerned about her was that her getting sick would draw attention to him, since they were seatmates and had taken all their meals together.

He ordered two roast beef sandwiches, an apple and a carton of milk to go. "I get hungry during the night, and we don't stop again until morning," he told Cara, who was looking askance at him, because he'd just stowed away a large steak, a double order of hash browns, salad and dessert.

An hour later, as darkness was beginning to creep across the highway, Bill nudged Cara. "I don't feel so good. I think maybe it's something I ate."

"Probably all that fried food," Cara said, nodding.

Bill reached down for the bag he'd placed at his feet. "Listen, I don't think I'm going to be able to eat this, and I hate to see food go to waste. Do you think you could at least eat some of it?"

"You might feel better after a bit," Cara said. She didn't take the bag.

He pushed it into her lap. "Please. I have a real horror about waste. I've seen too many kids starving all over the world."

Cara gave him a suspicious look, but then opened the bag and looked inside. "Well, all right, maybe I'll eat part of a sandwich and drink the milk."

She ate daintily, but he could see she was really hungry. When he saw how eagerly she drank the milk, he wished he'd bought two cartons.

"You've been all over the world?" Cara asked, as if his comment had just now registered with her.

"Yeah." Bill shifted uncomfortably in his seat. This was exactly why it was so dangerous to get next to people—the unthinking way information just popped out of one's mouth.

"Like where?" She took another bite of sandwich, and a tiny bit of mayo stuck to the corner of her mouth. Bill looked away, uneasy about his desire to reach over and lift it off with his finger. When he looked back, Cara was dabbing at her mouth with a paper napkin.

"Do you mind if we don't talk right now?" he said, dodging her question. "I'm really tired."

He hated the hurt that appeared in the girl's eyes. Hated that he cared whether he hurt her or not. If he was going to stay alive, to outsmart Alvaretti, he'd have to play by Alvaretti's rules. And the first one was, take care of number one and don't give a damn about anyone else.

He crossed his arms over his chest and closed his eyes, feigning sleep. After a few minutes, he dozed off for real.

THE IRON DOOR clanged shut with a threatening sound as Deacon Avery entered the small barred room where he was to meet with his client. There was a scarred rectangular wooden table with a chair at each end in the center of the room. Other than an ashtray in the middle of the table, there were no amenities in the space allotted for lawyer-client visits.

Deacon hated the room, the prison, the trips upstate. But when Franco Alvaretti sent for you, you didn't argue and you didn't delay. Even though Franco was in prison, he was still a formidable enemy.

He took out a cigarette and then put it back, remembering that Franco had hated smoking ever since he, himself, had given up the expensive cigars he once smoked endlessly. Deacon went to the window and winced at the barren scene below: a huge concrete-walled exercise yard that seemed to exemplify—even more than the barred doors and windows—the emptiness of prison life.

He stroked his cigarette pack and hoped this meeting would be brief. He wondered what could be keeping Franco.

As if in response to his thoughts, he heard the now-familiar sound of a key grating in a lock, and then a door on the opposite wall opened to reveal Deacon's client and, behind him, an armed guard.

"You got ten minutes, Franco," the guard warned, in a pleasant voice. Deacon knew instantly that this was one of the guards who were now on the Alvaretti payroll.

"Deke, good to see you, old friend," Franco called out, holding his arms open to Deacon.

They hugged briefly in the traditional manner, and then Deacon went to the table and lifted his briefcase onto its surface. "We don't have much time, Franco. Maybe you want to get right down to business."

Franco put his hand out to prevent Deacon from opening the case. "This is a different kind of business, Deke. You won't need anything in there."

Deacon let his surprise show in his expression. He had assumed this was going to be a discussion of the business and the delegation of authority during Franco's incarceration.

Franco shook his head. "This is personal, Deke, and I figure you're indebted enough to me that you'll carry out my orders."

Deacon shifted uncomfortably in his chair. "I've always followed your orders, Franco, you know that."

"Good," Franco said with a nod. "Then let's cut right to the chase, as they say. Where is Bill Spencer?"

Deacon blinked and stared at Franco, aghast. "Why would you think I'd know that, Franco? We know he must have gone underground, probably with the WPP's help, but I certainly have no knowledge of his location."

"Then find out!"

"I beg your pardon?"

"I said, find him. And do it now! The longer you delay, the more apt you are to lose him for good."

"But why would—?"

"I want him wasted."

Deacon blanched and gripped the table edge as a dizzy spell threatened. "Franco... it's over... Why don't you just forget—"

The other man leaped to his feet, knocking the chair over. "Don't tell me to forget, Deacon. You're not the one stuck in this place for the next twenty years, with nothing to do but remember your enemies. Or maybe," he began, leaning forward and grabbing Deacon's jacket lapel, his face just inches from Deacon's, "you're one of them?"

"No! No way, Franco, you know I'm with you... all the way, Franco."

Deacon could feel the sweat forming on his face, behind his ears, under his arms and between his thighs.

As quickly as he'd lost his temper, Franco's good humor was restored. He picked up his chair and sat down, smiling at Deacon.

"Good. Now, use all the people you need to locate Spencer, and then, when that's accomplished, get in touch with me."

"You want me to send out an...enforcer, Franco?"

"No. Just find him. I'll tell you what to do once I know you've got him in your sights."

He stood up and reached across the table to pat Deacon's cheek affectionately. "Don't get your marbles in an uproar, Deke. I'm not going to make you pull the trigger."

His laughter echoed back to Deacon long after the guard had led Alvaretti out of the room. It took Deacon a few minutes to wipe the sweat from his face and stop his hand from shaking so that he could press the buzzer to summon a guard to let him out.

Chapter Two

Cara finished the food in the bag while Bill slept. It was too dark by then to see anything outside the windows, and she closed her eyes and thought about how lucky it had been that Bill felt too ill to eat the food he'd purchased. She had been so hungry, she'd been on the verge of feeling sick herself. But she had limited funds, and she had to make them stretch. She couldn't afford to blow all her money on meals in restaurants.

When she got where she was going, and got her own place, she'd stock up on cheap things like bread and luncheon meat. She'd live on that just fine until she had money coming in. Maybe she'd land a job in a restaurant where they'd provide some of her meals.

A spasm of despair gripped her; all those years of working toward her M.B.A. and now she would be reduced to working as a waitress or something. She sighed. She couldn't let herself suffer remorse now—she'd made her decision and followed through on it. This was no time to be feeling sorry for herself.

She glanced over at Bill Hamlin, hoping her restlessness hadn't disturbed his sleep. His breathing was shallow and even, and his face was more handsome when he was at peace, not wearing its usual expression of wariness.

It occurred to her that they'd been on the bus together for about eighteen hours, and he didn't look the least bit rumpled or disheveled. Maybe that was a trick a world traveler learned. Ruefully she looked down at her own outfit, which wasn't holding up well at all. In the morning she'd go into the ladies' room and change into one of her other outfits, though she suspected they'd be pretty wrinkled, too, from being folded in the gym bag.

Her reflection in the night-darkened window told her that her hair needed a good brushing and any sign of lipstick was gone.

Funny that a man who had traveled all over the world would end up riding on a cross-country bus, she mused, closing her eyes again. But then, she'd read about people who made treks on foot or by bicycle, sleeping in barns and hostels and living out of their backpacks. Maybe Bill Hamlin was one of those.

She took a deep breath. He sure did smell good. It couldn't be aftershave, she realized, opening one eye to peek at him. He had a beard. Must be hair oil, or some kind of scented men's soap.

It made her think of Doug, and she winced and folded her arms around her body. She didn't have to worry about Doug anymore, or about her mother. Even if her mother should decide to hire someone to find her, she was pretty sure she could avoid discovery. When her car was found, they'd think she was somewhere in Boston.

A tiny prickle of fear shot through her. What if they thought she'd been killed? Her mother would never rest until her body was found and the murderer put in jail.

What body? What murderer? Giving a soft chuckle, Cara realized that scenario would never be played out.

And then, suddenly, humor turned to sorrow and, despite her determination to avoid self-pity, she began to cry quietly, missing her mother, her home, wishing things could have been different, wishing Doug had never come into their lives.

"Hey," Bill said softly, turning his head to look at her. "Are you crying?"

"No." She shook her head and dashed the tears from her eyes. "I thought you were asleep," she said, her voice muffled, as she looked through her purse for tissues.

"I'm a light sleeper. When the person next to me starts to cry, I usually wake up."

He handed her one of those small packages of tissue that were sold at checkout counters. Cara took one and blew her nose into it, handing the packet back to him.

"Keep it. I suspect the waterworks aren't over yet."

A fresh flood of tears proved him right. Cara leaned against the window and wept quietly.

Beside her, Bill Hamlin sat quite still, not touching her, not pretending to understand her pain or attempting to talk her out of her distress.

Cara wiped her eyes and nose and turned to him with a look of wry reproach. "You've done this before," she said accusingly.

"You mean waited for some damsel in distress to get over the boo-hoos?"

Cara grinned in spite of herself and then nodded.

Bill stretched his legs, slouched on his spine and turned his head toward her. "If you ask a woman why she's crying, she invariably either says she isn't or that it's nothing. If you try to comfort her, you can't possibly find the words that will make any difference. And if you try to touch her, you either get shrugged off, punched, or drenched from the tears. I've learned it's better to wait it out.''

Cara laughed. ''Thanks.''

Bill smiled. It was a strangely gentle, compassionate smile, Cara thought.

''It's okay. We all have periods when we want to go into a corner and bawl.''

''Not men,'' Cara said firmly.

''Oho! You don't know much about men, apparently.''

Cara studied her seatmate with renewed interest, her own loneliness forgotten. He certainly didn't look the type to cry. But then, what would that type look like? Effeminate? The man beside her was hardly that.

''I ate all your food,'' she said.

''I hoped you would,'' he replied.

''It...I...''

''You were hungry.'' Bill nodded. ''It's okay, I understand. I've been there a time or two myself.''

Cara was grateful that he'd relieved her of the awkwardness of having to explain her limited finances, but she didn't want him to pity her, either.

''I could use my money for food, but I need it more for something else.''

Again Bill nodded. ''Sure. Don't worry about it. And if you're a good seatmate and don't snore while you sleep, I'll buy you breakfast in the morning as a reward.''

''I don't snore,'' Cara said indignantly.

Bill folded his arms across his chest and closed his eyes. ''Good,'' he said, smiling wearily. ''Then you're a shoo-in for the superdeluxe ranch steak and eggs special.''

Cara laughed and made herself as comfortable as she could beside Bill. What a nice man. And without any hint of flirtatiousness. He reminded her of her father, though he was younger than her father had been when he died. Come to think of it, he must be about Doug's age, halfway between her mother and herself.

But she mustn't think about the people at home; if she did, she'd start crying again.

She decided to think about breakfast with Bill, instead. She smiled at the thought. She'd use the ladies' room and change into jeans and her pink long-sleeved knit shirt. Jeans held up better for travel. And she'd put on a little makeup and fix her hair. She wasn't going to give him a single reason to regret inviting her to breakfast.

She was almost asleep when his head slipped onto her shoulder. Cara held her breath, her body rigid, but then relaxed. It was nice having him there, she decided; familiar and not at all threatening.

DOUG HARVARD fought for control as Beth Dunlap paced the floor, wringing her hands and weeping noisily.

"I can't believe she just took off like that, sneaking away in the dark of night without even telling me she was leaving."

"She did leave a note, darling," Doug reminded her gently.

"Maybe I should notify the police, report her missing." Beth's voice had strengthened, the teariness giving way to resolve.

"Darling, the police would say she left on her own, that she isn't really missing."

"What about a private detective, then?"

It was time to bring Beth back under control. Doug went to her and enfolded her in his arms, holding her head against his chest, soothingly rubbing her back.

"Listen, my dear, Cara is a grown woman, not a runaway child. Why don't we give her time to get settled wherever she's gone, and then, if we don't hear from her in, say—oh, a month—we'll talk about looking for her? Meanwhile—" he lowered his voice seductively and lifted her chin so that he could gaze into her eyes "—why don't we take advantage of our newfound privacy and get married right away."

Beth gasped. "Right away? You mean—?"

Doug nodded and gave her a practiced smile, heavy with promise. "I mean tomorrow. We already have the license, and with Cara gone, we don't have any family to cater to. Let's just go off by ourselves and exchange our vows privately." He brushed her lips with his own. "It would be so much more romantic, my love," he whispered.

"What about my friends?" Beth protested weakly. "They'll be so disappointed."

Doug's hands moved from Beth's back to just under her breasts. He held back a smile of satisfaction when Beth gave a tremulous gasp of excitement. "I'll be even more disappointed if I have to wait one more night to make you my wife," he said, making his voice rough.

"We don't have to wait," Beth said, moving closer, rubbing her pelvis against Doug's. "I've always told you I'd be willing to make love with you before the wedding. After all," she added archly, "I'm a woman of the nineties."

Damned near, Doug thought. But he said, "No, darling, as I've told you so often before, I need to know you're all mine, entirely committed to me, and I to you, before I can accept that last, most wondrous gift from you."

He let his fingers graze her nipples, almost as if by mistake, and had the satisfaction of hearing her moan of desire as she ground her hips against him in desperation.

He drew away, his expression one of deep regret. "Don't make me wait any longer, Beth darling, please. I need you so." He put his hand to his fly and clutched himself in seeming pain. "Please, darling, say you'll marry me tomorrow, and let's start our honeymoon now, tonight."

He could see she'd had all she could take of his sexual game of cat and mouse. His offer to put the honeymoon before the wedding was the clincher. She fell into his arms, almost tearing his shirt open, and agreed to marry him the next day.

Doug called on his favorite fantasy in order to prepare for the night ahead. Cara Dunlap might have gotten away from him in fact, but in his mind he could still have his way with her, and visualizing breaking her to his will was exciting enough to allow him to perform like a passion-crazed bridegroom.

Hours later, as Beth slept beside him, Doug lay in the darkened master bedroom and eased himself into sleep by working out the details for making Beth Dunlap's fortune his own.

"WE'RE HALFWAY THERE," Bill said as he slid into the booth across from Cara. "The driver says we're right on schedule."

Cara put down the menu she'd been studying. "Are you going to be staying in San Francisco for a while?"

Bill gave her a strange look. "No," he said, in a tone that prohibited further questions.

Cara wriggled uncomfortably and frowned. "I just thought, since I don't know anyone there, it would be nice..."

"Look, kid, when this trip is over, we're history. I travel fast and I travel alone, and I don't take on any cargo along the way."

Cara flushed. "I'm not a kid, for one thing, Bill Hamlin, and I wasn't suggesting you 'take me on,' so you can drop the Humphrey Bogart routine. I just thought it would be nice to know there was someone I knew in the same city with me while I'm getting settled."

He hadn't meant to snap at her like that, and he knew he'd sounded like a real jerk. But as the hours they spent together sped by, he was beginning to feel more and more at risk. There was something so compelling about her— a combination of vulnerability and recklessness. Something in him yearned to reach out and either shake her or grab her and hold her tight. And that was exactly the kind of emotional involvement that could make him lose sight of his own safety concerns, make him careless.

They had another day and a half on the bus, another night of falling asleep smelling her shampoo, her sweet, clean fragrance, feeling her arm against his, her leg brushing his when she turned to say something to him. He was, first and foremost a man, one who hadn't held a woman in longer than he cared to remember. It might be years before it was safe for him to get involved again— if ever—but while they were traveling across the country, suspended in the limbo of continuous movement, he could almost pretend they were just two normal people who were on the verge of becoming friends.

"Order something filling," he said gruffly to Cara. "And don't be so thin-skinned. I didn't mean to insult you."

He hid a smile behind his menu. He could tell from the play of emotions he'd seen across her face that she was torn between indignation and hunger.

She ordered eggs and pancakes and a large glass of milk.

"That's more like it," Bill said, nodding in approval. "Now, let's talk about you. What are you going to do in San Francisco?"

He had a day and a half in which to enjoy this young woman's company. He decided that as long as he was on the bus it was safe for him to let his guard down enough to make it a congenial trip. She intrigued him, with her soft prettiness, her feisty temper, her hint of sad mystery. He would have liked to encourage her to reveal the source of that mystery but he knew that if he did, she'd feel justified in questioning him in return. He couldn't have that.

Cara played with her cutlery and looked out the window of the café, staring off into the distance, where the desert met the horizon like a great sand-colored ocean.

"Look for a job, a place to live," she said dreamily. "Start a new life."

"Wipe out the old one," Bill said, almost to himself.

"What?" Cara returned her gaze to Bill, startled by his remark. How could she respond to that? How could she tell a stranger about her mother's obsession with a younger man whose own obsession was with her daughter? How could she explain the guilt, the shame, she felt every time she entered a room with her mother and Doug in it. And, worst of all, how could she explain how Doug had manipulated her with emotional blackmail, knowing she wouldn't be able to bear to hurt her mother by telling her the truth about the man her mother loved?

"I...I just felt the need to try someplace new," she said weakly.

"And you're traveling clear across the country to find it?"

Cara nodded and returned her gaze to the window.

Doug was going to be furious when he discovered she'd finally found the courage to escape his advances. Would he look for her, risk losing her mother? She prayed that her opinion of Doug was correct, that he was just a bit more obsessed with her mother's money than he was with Cara, that that little edge might keep him in Greensville, keep him from looking for her.

She pushed away the stab of guilt she felt over leaving her mother at Doug's mercy. She'd turned the situation over in her mind, considered her options, made her choice. She'd live by it.

Their food arrived before Bill could ply her with more questions. Cara picked up her fork almost before the waitress set her plate down, glad for the diversion and for the bounty of food before her.

They were almost finished with the meal when the driver came in and called for everyone's attention.

"We're going to have a slight delay, folks. Nothing to worry about, but you're going to have a couple of extra hours here, so take your time and enjoy the scenery. If you want to go for walks or look around the town, be sure you're back by ten."

"Oh, let's go for a walk," Cara said, excited at the prospect of seeing something of the countryside that was passing by her almost as soon as her gaze fell on it.

Bill studied her face, enjoying the flush of excitement in her cheeks, the shine in her eyes. Great eyes, he thought. Not just dark brown, but more the color of burned caramel. They glinted with golden lights every time her face changed expression.

He glanced out at the parking lot. Apart from three Greyhound buses, there was an eighteen-wheeler, a pickup truck with a load of vegetables in the back, and two compact cars. He looked around the café. Nobody who could remotely be connected with the mob.

He looked back at Cara, whose smile was beguiling. "Okay, you're on," he said, rising and throwing a couple of bills on the food check.

But as they were strolling the streets of the small town, Bill was already beginning to question the reckless manner in which he was getting involved with this girl. Something about her tugged at him, at some long-buried part of him that preceded his years in the Service, his brief but disastrous marriage, even the pseudocynical years of college. She took him back to his true beginnings, to halcyon days of family and growing up in middle America with nothing to threaten the peace but the seasonal attacks of weather.

It was that life, hidden away from the rest of the country, that had made him want to make a career out of defending and protecting the things he loved and believed in.

"Look at that," Cara said breathlessly, pointing to the mountain rise that suddenly appeared out of nowhere, making a magnificent backdrop for the row of low buildings they'd come upon.

"Makes a person feel . . . insignificant," Bill said, absorbing the feeling as he stared at the mountain.

"Because it's been there forever and will be there forever," Cara stated solemnly. She turned from the awe-inspiring sight and looked up at her companion.

"Doesn't it make you want to stay right here and let it stand guard over your life?"

Bill glanced at Cara and then back at the mountain, shaking his head. "There are some things it can't protect you from. There are people out there who would never stop to look at that mountain, never notice its beauty or its magnificence. People who wouldn't hesitate to blow up the mountain if it stood in the way of what they wanted to achieve."

Cara stared at Bill, aghast. She'd never heard such cynical talk before, never heard that note of utter futility in another person's voice.

She would have liked to probe, to find out what it was that had made this man so bitter; it was a sharp contrast to the gentle, generous man he'd shown her.

But there was also a dark aspect to his nature, one that warned her that she must not overstep certain boundaries in their brief, temporary relationship.

"Even if all that's true, it doesn't keep us from enjoying the beauty," she said, and turned away from the view. "It must be nearly time to head back," she added quietly.

He fell into step beside her, and they remained silent, both lost in their own thoughts, on the walk back.

The silence continued, almost by mutual consent, for the next leg of their journey. When they stopped for lunch, Cara pleaded a headache as an excuse for not joining Bill in the café.

"Just bring me back some coffee, please," she said, handing him a dollar bill.

He gave her a skeptical look, but didn't argue. He just took her money and nodded.

Cara laid her head against the window and let her eyes close against the noon sunshine. Something about Bill

Hamlin's carefully guarded pain had struck a chord in Cara and made the reality of her situation all the more frightening. It wasn't that she wasn't capable of fending for herself or being alone. After all, she was an only child, whose parents had been loving and giving, but also very involved with one another.

Her father had become ill when she graduated from high school, and despite his protests, she'd put off going to college in order to spend as much time with him as his illness would allow. The shared nursing duties, plus the feeling of pending doom in the house, had brought Cara and her mother closer.

But after her father's death, her mother had shut Cara out while she mourned the loss of her husband. And Cara had gone off to start her college years, feeling orphaned and lonely, so that even though she was a couple of years older than the other freshmen, she seemed younger, shier. It had taken her a full year to get past her own grief and begin to make friends and enjoy the campus ambience.

By the time Cara's mother came out of mourning, Cara had already been in her last year of graduate school. A few months later, Doug had come into their lives.

No, the problem wasn't encroaching loneliness—that was an emotion she'd lived with most of her life. It was more the reminder that she was leaving everything she'd considered safe and familiar and was about to enter a strange world without access to any of the comforts of her past, and where she couldn't even use her given name. Could she carve out a niche for herself while living like an illegal alien? And was the sacrifice she was making worthwhile?

Because of her parents' obvious closeness, she'd grown up believing that the biggest event in her life was going to be falling in love and becoming a wife and mother. Only in her case, she'd planned to love her husband and her children equally, so that none of them ever felt left out.

Was such a future possible for her now? Could she be legally married under an assumed name? And where would she meet the ideal man, if she was forced to take odd jobs that didn't require references or close scrutiny of her qualifications?

Her reverie was interrupted by Bill's return. He handed her a bag that obviously contained something more than the cup of coffee she'd asked for.

"You'll feel hungry later," he said, shrugging off her protest. "Did you take some aspirin for that headache?"

Cara nodded, avoiding his eyes so that he couldn't see the lie. She was sure she could have told him the truth, that she had just wanted to be alone, but then he might have asked questions she wasn't prepared to answer.

What would a man who was as obviously worldly as Bill Hamlin think of her sordid story? Would he believe she was an innocent victim, or would he think she'd come on to her mother's boyfriend and invited his attentions?

"Better drink that coffee before it gets cold," Bill said as he adjusted his seat to a reclining position.

Cara nodded and opened the bag to find it contained a sandwich and a banana, as well as a cup of coffee.

"You missed your calling, Bill." She grinned over at him. "You should have been a nutritionist."

He didn't smile in response. His face was set in a hostile mask, and his voice held a quiet threat as he asked, "What makes you think I'm not? And what do you know about my calling?"

Cara might have snapped back at him, if just at that moment the bus hadn't lurched to the side and then come to an abrupt halt with a terrible screeching of the brakes.

Chapter Three

The driver used his radiophone to call in the broken axle. Within thirty minutes, the motel in Mount View, the town they had just come from, sent out its minivan to start hauling passengers back. The local garage sent a tow truck. The driver announced that a replacement bus would arrive in the morning, and in the meantime the motel would put up the passengers at the bus company's expense.

Cara was on the first trek the van made, and she waited in the motel lobby with the others until the entire bus-load had arrived and were assigned rooms.

She passed the time looking over the postcard rack in the lobby, looking for a card to send her mother, just to let her know that she was safe. After all, it wasn't as if they were staying in Mount View. They'd be long gone before Beth Dunlap ever received the card.

She chose one with a picture of the mountains and wrote a brief message, saying not to worry, that she was fine and enjoying traveling around the country.

She then curled up in the corner of one of the couches with her journal and a cup of coffee and a doughnut and wrote down everything she was feeling in a sort of letter to her mother.

She had just tucked the journal back into her gym bag when the last of her fellow passengers arrived, with Bill in their midst.

There were a few questions and some grumbling from the other passengers, but most took the news in stride, enjoying the diversion of a little adventure and the prospect of a night's sleep in a real bed. They lined up at the desk to get their keys in orderly fashion. Cara found herself beside Bill.

"How about a swim before dinner?" Bill suggested.

Cara's face brightened, then fell. "I didn't bring a suit."

Bill nodded and looked away as the line moved.

"But if that's an invitation to dinner, I accept," Cara said, putting a hand on his arm to get his attention. She jumped back when something like a wave of electricity jolted up her arm. Bill seemed similarly afflicted.

"Sorry," she muttered, "must be the carp—"

Simultaneously they glanced down at the red tile floor and then lifted their eyes, meeting query with confusion.

"I do like a woman with spark," Bill said, in a near whisper. His eyes gleamed, and a little muscle twitched along his jaw as he gave his full attention to her face.

Cara could feel his roving gaze, like a warm hand lightly caressing her skin. Her own eyes were drawn to the angles and planes of his face, to the full curve of his lips, the hard edge of his cheekbones. When she tried to swallow, her throat felt dry.

The bus driver called out, "Keep moving, folks," and Cara and Bill returned to the present.

Cara soon found herself at the desk, and had to think a moment when the desk clerk asked her name. She went through the business of registering, finding her room and unpacking her few items of clothing with a soft smile on her lips. She'd seen a liquor store at the other end of the street, across from the motel, and decided she'd spend a little of her nest egg to provide a bottle of dessert wine as a way of thanking Bill for the dinner and the other meals he'd provided her. She tried not to ask herself why this particular meal felt like a date, after all the other, casual meals they'd shared on the trip. Bill had certainly made it clear that his only interest in her was as a seat partner for the duration of the journey. For herself, she wasn't even sure Bill Hamlin was the type she would have dated if she'd met him under other circumstances.

Yet the memory of that moment in the lobby, when they'd looked deep into one another's eyes, still had the power to steal her breath away and bring heat to the surface of her skin. Her type or not, he was the most damnably attractive man she'd ever met, and for tonight, at least, she intended to enjoy the pretense that he was a real dinner date and that they were on the verge of something sweet and promising—not to mention something dangerous and compelling.

BILL WENT TO HIS ROOM, changed into swim trunks and headed for the pool. He'd always used swimming for his fitness regimen, since his career had entailed so much travel, and most hotels and motels had pools. This one echoed with the lack of bodies at this time of day, and Bill reveled in having the place to himself.

He dived in and then found that it took him a few minutes to get oriented. For some reason, the warm, silken water on his skin made him think of Cara. He'd never thought of swimming as an exercise in the erotic, but now he found himself wishing that Cara had been able to join him. He envisioned her long-limbed slenderness in a French-cut swimsuit, and the fantasy shortened his breath and made his limbs tense with desire. He could see her stroking beside him, her arms golden as they flashed through the water, her head tilted to the side as they stared into one another's eyes.

He squeezed his eyes shut and forced his breathing into a rhythm his body could follow. He had no business thinking about Cara Davis in that way. For that matter, when had he begun to think of her as a desirable woman, rather than a casual traveling companion? It must have something to do with the fact that this was a sort of reprieve in the midst of his desperate journey. One night, suspended in time, to allow them to pretend they were normal people who'd happened to meet on a bus and were drawn to one another because they were young, attractive and available.

I'm not available, he reminded himself.

And it didn't matter when his perception of her had changed. The point was that it was self-defeating to allow himself the diversion, and he was going to have to get control over such errant thoughts.

He did punishing laps for exercise and then leisurely breaststroked around the perimeter of the pool a couple of times. By the time he hoisted himself up onto the ceramic deck, his endorphins were humming and he felt physically better than he had in days.

He didn't know why, but he felt safe here. Safe enough to look forward to his evening with his lovely traveling companion. There would be time enough tomorrow to restore the necessary status quo.

He whistled jauntily as he started down the carpeted hall to his room, and then he stopped dead in his tracks when he spotted Cara at the end of the corridor in front of the ice machine. She was talking to some man—a man Bill didn't recognize from the bus—and the way they had their heads together, it was obvious to Bill that they were discussing something serious. Acting on instinct, he stepped back and flattened himself against the wall around the corner.

He waited a couple of minutes and then eased out to the edge of the wall and looked down the hall. Cara and the man were gone.

Bill took a deep breath and went on to his room. Okay, so his seatmate was talking to some guy. So what? She was a pretty girl; men were apt to notice her, hit on her. It was none of his business.

It made him uncomfortable to realize that if the man had been young and good-looking, what he was feeling might have been dubbed jealousy.

He made himself focus on their dinner date. He'd asked at the desk and been told there were actually four good places to choose from, since this was on a main route through the mountains, and many tourists stopped to enjoy the view.

He was dressed in record time, and too restless to wait in his room. According to his watch, it was a good hour before most dining rooms would open for dinner. He decided to let Cara know he was going for a stroll around the grounds and would meet her in the lobby in an hour.

THEY DINED at a table in the corner of the dining room of the Mount View Inn, which was large enough to allow them some privacy, though there were other dinner guests scattered throughout the room. Candles flickered, flowers scented the air, and soft music played through speakers strategically placed on each wall.

Bill and Cara faced each other across white linen, self-consciously holding large menus in front of them.

"You look lovely, Cara," Bill said at last, setting his menu down with a sigh.

"I was just thinking that this room merits something dressier than a skirt and sweater," Cara shyly replied, peeking around her menu.

"I think it's more than just your outfit. I like your hair like that, by the way."

"Thank you." She'd pulled her hair up into a cluster of curls atop her head and used slightly more makeup than usual. "You look nice, too, Bill," she said, and ducked back behind the menu as she felt a warm flush move up into her face.

Bill chuckled. "Must be the altitude," he said.

"What?"

"This self-consciousness between us. Either that, or we're just truck-stop people at heart."

"I'd never been in a truck stop before I came on this trip," Cara said. She didn't add that dining rooms like this were much more in her league.

"No? Well, as a matter of fact, I'm more used to bistros and hotel dining rooms, myself."

"Bistros. That would be Europe, right?"

Bill appeared to weigh his answer before nodding.

"Yeah. Mostly."

"I've never been abroad, but I always knew I'd get there someday." Her face fell. "Maybe not now."

"Why not now?"

Cara shrugged. "I guess I just see a different kind of future than I used to expect."

The waiter came to their table just then, and they both ordered the crab legs. Bill ordered a sauvignon blanc to go with their meal, and Cara smiled inwardly, pleased to discover that he liked wine.

"You like crab legs, too," Bill said.

"Mm-hmm." Cara sipped from her water goblet. "I'm a true New Englander." That raised a question she couldn't help but ask. "Where are you from?" The look on his face caused her to amend her question hurriedly. "I mean originally."

She watched the play of emotions alter his face, and she thought he must be considering how much he could tell her.

She could see he was telling the truth when he finally answered, "A small town in the Midwest." It wasn't much, but it was a start—an opening-up to her, which he'd obviously been avoiding.

"Small towns are nice," she said, reaching for a roll just to have something to do with her hands.

"They are. There is something so rich about life in a small town." His voice and eyes became dreamy. "People really live with one another, really share their lives. In big cities, people just live side by side, their lives not really touching."

"That's... profound, Bill. And very true, I think."

She concentrated on buttering her bread for a moment before asking, "Do you get home often?"

"Home?" Bill busied himself with a roll of his own. "There is no home any longer. My family was small and short-lived and—" He shifted in his seat, obviously uncomfortable. "Listen, do you mind if we change the subject?"

"No, of course not, Bill. I'm sorry." She frowned and looked away.

She jumped and turned back when she felt Bill's hand close around hers, where it rested on the table.

"Hey, darlin'? Don't take my bad manners so personally, okay?" His eyes beseeched understanding, and his hand was warm on hers. She fought the impulse to turn her hand so that their palms touched.

She sought a new topic of conversation, instead. "This town reminds me of one of my favorite movies."

"Oh? Which?"

"Continental Divide."

"Ah, John Belushi and Blair Brown."

Cara's hand turned of its own accord.

"You know the movie?" She felt their palms meet and started to draw away, but his fingers closed around hers.

Bill grinned. "It's my secret vice. Movies. And that was a favorite of mine, because of the ending."

"I thought the ending was a little disappointing."

"You didn't think it was a happy ending?"

"Yes and no. It didn't really let you know how they were going to live out their lives, when her work kept her in the mountains and his kept him in the city."

"You like every *t* crossed and every *i* dotted."

Their hands seemed to have acquired a life of their own. It was almost as though their hearts were beating in unison, right there between their palms. "It's not that," she said, reaching for her water glass with her free hand. She took a nervous gulp. The glass wobbled as she set it on the tabletop again. "It's more a need to know that the hero and heroine are going to make it."

"There's more than one way to make it," Bill said, leaning forward, his voice hushed and slightly husky. "And that's what that movie says, and why I liked it." The candlelight was reflected in his dark blue eyes, and it softened the planes of his face. Cara felt the pulse in her throat begin to quicken.

"Salads, sir?" The salad cart bumped against their table, and Bill and Cara jumped apart.

"Yes, th-thanks," Bill stammered. Cara was delighted to discover that her sophisticated traveling companion was capable of being rattled. It gave her a slight edge, she thought.

It was an argument about white hats and black hats that brought them back to reality. "No, it's not always like that," Bill said, when Cara insisted that the white hats were always the good guys and always won. "At least not in the real world."

He seemed to lose some of his energy after that and when he signaled for the bill, Cara didn't protest.

They were silent on the way back to the motel. *I don't want it to end,* she thought. But she knew it had to, had known all along that this was never going to last beyond tonight, or at the most beyond their arrival in San Francisco, when they would go their separate ways.

But tonight wasn't really over, she reminded herself as they passed the now-darkened liquor store. She'd surprise him with the wine she'd purchased earlier, and maybe they could recapture some of the good feelings they'd shared during dinner. They could talk all night. It didn't matter. They could sleep all the next day on the bus.

They were just entering the lobby when the elevator doors opened, revealing a lone man within the car.

It was the man from the ice machine. Cara started to raise her hand, but the man looked startled to see them and quickly jabbed the button that caused the elevator doors to close.

"What was that all about?" Bill asked, a frown creasing his forehead.

Cara shrugged. "I don't know," she said. "I guess he thought this was his floor."

"Do you know him?"

"Know him? No. Why would you think that?"

"Oh, no reason. I just thought you looked like you recognized him."

"Oh. Well, I did talk to him briefly at the ice machine. He needed directions."

"Funny, he didn't seem anxious to recognize you just now."

"Well, I only talked to him for a moment. Maybe he didn't recognize me."

"Maybe." But Bill looked dubious. Cara might have questioned him, but she decided what she wanted most was to restore the mood they'd shared earlier. Just then the elevator car returned to the main floor and the doors drew apart. This time the car was vacant.

"I enjoyed dinner, Bill," she said, as they entered the elevator.

"Yeah, that was fun. I'll have to thank the desk clerk for suggesting the inn."

They got off on the third floor and walked down the hall to Cara's room. Bill waited while Cara got her room key out of her purse and unlocked the door. She turned around and smiled. "See you later, Bill, and thanks again."

"Sure. My pleasure."

He hesitated a moment, and Cara thought he was going to kiss her. Her hand grasped the edge of the door nervously. But he merely nodded and turned away, headed for his own room.

Cara went inside and closed the door. She'd give him a few minutes to get settled and then surprise him with the wine.

BILL WAS JUST PACKING his sport coat when a knock came at the door. He stood at the door and breathed deeply before asking, "Who is it?"

"It's me, Bill. Cara."

He opened the door.

"Cara." He stared at her, clearly shocked.

She lifted her hands and he saw that she was holding an ice bucket in one hand and a brown paper bag in the other. "Aren't you going to invite me in?"

"Cara...do you think this is a good idea? I mean..."

Cara laughed. "Gosh, Bill, you don't have to look like I've come to strip you of your virginity. Here, I bought this earlier, thought we could extend the evening a little with a nightcap." She moved past him, set the bag down on the desk and pulled out the wine.

He should have been impressed that she'd made such a gesture. Instead, an image of Cara and the stranger came into his mind, followed by an image of himself drunk and Cara and the man bending over his helpless form.

His mind went into overdrive. She was taking glasses from the tray on the desk, putting ice into them, and her back was to him.

Swiftly he pulled his belt from the loops of his pants and banded it around Cara's upper body, imprisoning her arms at her sides. The element of surprise kept her silent long enough for him to gag her with a washcloth. A moment later, he had her in the desk chair and was using his tie to secure her ankles to the chair legs.

She attempted to speak, but the gag stifled the sound, and Bill kept working methodically, ignoring her pleas.

She must have been a plant, he told himself. Alvaretti's people must have somehow located him and sent her to make sure. The guy in the elevator was probably her contact.

Bill's hands trembled as he made one last knot. He hadn't even been on the run a week, and already they'd found him. Alvaretti's posse would probably be showing up next. He wondered how much time he had.

He got to his feet and looked down at the girl. Her eyes were wide, dark with pleading. He forced himself to look away. "Sorry, darlin', but better you than me."

He was packed and out the door in minutes, grabbing Cara's room key off the desk, where she'd set it down when she started to fix the drinks. There'd be something in her things to show him who she really was, who her contact was, what their plans for him were. Something to show him what his next move should be.

He made a rapid, efficient sweep of her room . . . and found nothing.

Nothing but a journal. He opened it to the last entry, planning to read back as far as he needed to find out the truth. He read the letter to her mother.

He sank to the bed as he read of Cara's dilemma. Of the way her mother's fiancé kept coming on to her, of how she loved her mother and couldn't bear to see her hurt. He read that she'd threatened to tell her mother the truth about Harvard and that he had warned her that he would say she was lying, speaking out of jealousy, that she was the one who wanted him. Cara's mother would believe her fiancé, because she was so enamored of him and since she was already angry that Cara didn't seem to approve of their upcoming nuptials.

He felt numb as he replaced her notebook in the small gym bag, noticing how pitifully few things she'd taken away with her. He was going to have to go back and untie her, explain why he'd gone nuts like that.

But he couldn't really tell her everything. She might be exactly what she appeared to be—a kind of heroine who would sacrifice her own life to spare her mother's pride—but he couldn't confide in her. For one thing, it would only put her at risk to know the truth. If Alvaretti's people connected him to her and began to question her, she'd be less of a threat if she knew nothing.

Maybe he'd do better to just move on, leave her where she was. The maid would find her in the morning. It wasn't like she was in danger. She'd be a little uncomfortable for a few hours, but that was all.

He slipped down the hall, staying in the shadows, and eased out the back door. Once outside, he headed for the saloon across from the motel, going around back, where the parking lot was located. He'd find a truck, get in back, and hitch a ride without the driver knowing he had a passenger.

There were no trucks back there, but it was early yet. By midnight the place would be jumping, and there were bound to be a couple of truckers among the revelers.

He huddled near the Dumpster behind the bar, trying to keep warm.

He must have dozed off. Male voices startled him into awareness. He smelled the unmistakable fragrance of marijuana smoke and heard one of the men inhale deeply and then exhale raggedly. "Don't hog it all," one of the men said harshly.

Bill was afraid this was going to turn into a long, drawn-out affair, but after a little conversation and a lot of smoke he finally heard the screeching sound of a metal door opening. For a moment, the noise in the bar could be plainly heard in the dark, otherwise silent night. And then the door clanged shut, and Bill knew he was alone again.

He was about to climb into the back of a semi when a vision of Cara snaked through his mind. *Had he tied her too tight?* He hefted one leg up onto the floor of the trailer, then hesitated. *What if she got thirsty with that terry-cloth rag in her mouth?* He hoisted his body up and turned to make sure no one had observed him getting into the truck. *By morning she'd be really cramped from sitting in that chair all night.* He stood up and started to slide the door shut.

He could see her face as clearly as if it were there in the darkened truck with him, the eyes so frightened they'd become dark as night.

BILL'S HEART thumped wildly as he tore across the street and ran through the lobby of the motel, not caring what others would think of his mad dash. He didn't know how he was going to explain his behavior to her, or what he'd do if she threatened to call the cops, which she had every right to do. He had to chance it. He just couldn't leave her tied up like that.

He didn't wait for the elevator, but took the stairs two at a time.

He felt as if the floor had dropped out from beneath his feet as he came to a panting halt in front of the open doorway to his empty room.

The chair where she should have been held captive had been replaced at the desk, and as his eyes scanned the room, he saw that his belt and necktie were neatly placed across the pillows on his bed.

Still disbelieving, he cautiously made his way into the room and crept over to the bathroom. Nothing. The room was neat as a pin, with no evidence of his earlier crime. The girl was gone, along with every sign that she'd been there. Even the two glasses she'd filled with ice were replaced on the tray on the desk, and the bottle of wine was gone.

He made the trip down to her room far more sedately than he'd reentered the motel. When he came to her door, he wiped his brow with the back of his arm before knocking.

He was prepared for anger, prepared for righteous indignation and outrage. He was even prepared for the cops to be lying in wait for him.

"Come in," a pleasant voice called out. "It's open."

He stood in the doorway and looked across the room to where she was seated at a table in front of the window, a floor lamp casting a soft glow across her hair and face.

She had a plastic glass of wine lifted to her lips. A crossword-puzzle book lay open in front of her.

"Hi, Bill," she said calmly.

"I...I..."

"You're just in time. Do you know a six-letter word for *dangerous?*" She picked up a pencil and held it poised over the puzzle page, an expectant look on her face.

"I'm...sorry."

She shook her head, and her silky hair flowed around her chin. "That's only five letters."

He cleared his throat. "I mean, I'm sorry, Cara. Honest to God, I'm really so sorry."

"Well, let's see," Cara said, meeting his pleading eyes with a steady look, "you attack me in your room as I'm attempting to pour us a glass of wine, and then you tie me to a chair and gag me, and then you go off and leave me there with no way to call for help. Did I miss anything?"

He didn't—couldn't—reply.

"No? Okay. Well, I guess that's everything. And now you say you're sorry. I'm sure you are. And indeed you should be," she said, in that same restrained manner.

And then, suddenly, she jumped up from the table, knocking her chair over, and ran at him.

"I thought you were some kind of perverted rapist, you big baboon!" she screamed, hitting him on the chest with both fists.

He barely felt the impact of her punches, so amazed was he by the amazing array of her emotions. This was no shrinking violet, no helpless little mama's girl, this . . . this *woman*.

It hit him with greater force than her fists. Cara Davis, or whatever her real name was, could be anything—a spy for Alvaretti, a government agent, a Sunday-school teacher, a runaway teenager. Anything she chose to portray, she could carry it off with aplomb. It wouldn't make it easier to trust her, but, by God, it certainly made it mandatory to respect her.

He grabbed her wrists, only to put an end to the chaotic melodrama. She couldn't get away, but he could feel how strong she was as she worked to break free of his greater strength.

"I thought you were on their side!" he yelled, shaking her slightly.

A sob caught in Cara's throat, and she stopped struggling. "Th-their side? Who are *they?*" The sob became a hiccup.

Bill opened his mouth to tell her and then realized he was right back where he'd begun. He couldn't tell her. He dropped her wrists.

"I can't explain. I just wanted you to know it was a mistake on my part and that I was only trying to protect myself."

She stared at him, squinting. "Protect yourself from me? Did you think I was going to poison the wine?"

"What?" He had to laugh, despite the seriousness of the situation. "No. Not from you. I mean, not from the wine. Well, yes, I guess I thought you were trying to get me drunk so you could..."

"Could what? Have my way with you?" He had to laugh with her at that. The eruption of laughter felt good.

It took a moment to remember their situation.

"Look, let's drop this. I can't tell you anything more, and I only came back because I thought it was wrong to leave you helpless like that."

Cara stepped back and grinned, holding her wrists up. "Helpless? Me? Ha!"

She marched back to the table, plunked down in her chair and picked up her wine. "Think again, big guy. Just because I'm having a few problems at home and I'm short on funds, that doesn't mean I'm some helpless little wimp. I can take care of myself—and, for that matter, I could probably do a better job of taking care of you than you're doing."

"What does that mean?" Bill demanded. What did she know? Who did she know?

"I mean, you seem to think that being a loner is the solution. I say, whoever *they* are, they're looking for a loner, a man on his own. With me at your side, you're part of a couple, and they aren't looking for a couple, are they?"

It was Bill's turn to stare. He went over and sank down on her bed, staring at her with his mouth ajar.

"A couple," he said, his voice heavy with awe.

"Right. Like a disguise. We'd be a disguise for one another. My people won't be looking for a couple, either."

Bill ran a hand through his hair and then shook his head, trying to clear it. The problem was that she made some sense, and that made no sense.

"Wait a minute," he said. "Less than an hour ago you thought I was a rapist—and, in fact, I did attack you and tie you up. Why should you trust me now."

And for that matter, why should I trust you? he thought.

"Or why should you trust me?"

"Are you a mind reader, too?"

Cara shrugged and shot him a complacent grin. "Isn't the enemy you know safer than the one you don't know?"

He had to grin, too, at her ridiculous logic. "I think I need that wine now."

He didn't wait for her response, but got up to pour it himself. With his back to her, he tried his thoughts out loud. "You're right about one thing—they know there hasn't been a woman in my life. They wouldn't expect me to be involved with anyone this quickly." He tilted his head back and drank some wine.

"For that matter... Wait a minute." He spun around. "Are you talking about a permanent arrangement?"

"Define *permanent*."

"Like for...weeks, months...whatever."

She nodded. "Wouldn't renting an apartment as a couple, looking for work as a couple, be good cover?"

Now he nodded, his expression thoughtful. "We're talking...um, separate bedrooms, of course."

"Of course."

"And you'd be willing to tie yourself down to me for the duration?"

"Better than you tying me to the nearest chair!"

Bill flinched, and Cara immediately regretted her sarcasm. "Sure, I'd trust you, Bill. You had second thoughts and came back to let me go, didn't you?"

Bill nodded and took a big gulp of wine. "Let me think this over."

He went to the door. "I'm going out to get us some coffee. I'm going to need a clear head to give your idea close consideration."

While he was gone, Cara peered through the drapes, waiting to see him emerge from the front of the motel. Her suggestion had been made out of the blue, without a lot of thought on her part. She really didn't know anything about him except that he was in terrible trouble, a lot worse than the trouble she'd run from. And she didn't even know if he was on the wrong side of the law. But even if he was, he meant no harm to her, she was sure, or else he wouldn't have come back to free her.

He came through the front door just then, and she looked down at the top of his head. Nice hair. And he had good carriage, the sort of thing her mother always noticed in people. She liked his easy stride and the natural way he stopped to look up and down the street. A casual bystander wouldn't guess he was checking to make sure it was safe.

Altogether, an attractive man, in a dark and dangerous way. Had she jumped from the frying pan into the fire? She remembered then the way her hand had felt in his, and the easy comfort of the hours they'd lingered over dinner...and she knew it was too late to change her mind.

Chapter Four

They were on their way to Santa Cruz.

"Close your eyes and point," Bill had ordered, holding a map of the Bay area in front of her.

It seemed a good omen that she'd hit on Santa Cruz. She'd become friendly with a woman on the bus who had a small baby. The woman had mentioned Santa Cruz in casual conversation. Cara wondered if she'd somehow been drawn to that spot on the map by suggestion, as if it were a kind of psychic magnet.

But, of course, she didn't share that thought with Bill. She was learning to guard her wayward thoughts from him. Words like *friend,* for example, seemed to have an adverse affect on him. The man trusted no one. Not even her, really. One wrong word or gesture and he became hostile and suspicious.

It was going to be interesting trying to live with a man who would find hidden meaning and threat in a wrong-number phone call or the need to run out for milk at eleven at night. Still, she was sure she was right about the situation being mutually beneficial for both of them, and now she could hardly wait to get there, to find an apartment and a job.

She glanced over at him, half hoping she'd catch a glimpse of a similar expression of excitement on his face. He had a great profile—strong, virile, resolute. But there was no sign of excitement. His jaw was set, and his eyes squinted slightly as he concentrated on the road.

Would it be possible to find a way to bring a little fun and fantasy into this guy's life? Cara mused. Right now, he was all mystery and menace, but she was sure that once they settled down and he felt safe from whoever "they" were he'd relax and show more humor.

Then her mind flashed back to the incident in San Francisco, and she knew Bill wouldn't find much humor in the secret she was harboring.

She'd had to wait for him at the Museum of Natural History while he took care of some mysterious business elsewhere. He had told her he was going to buy a car, among other things, so that they could drive to Santa Cruz.

She'd wandered from exhibit to exhibit, but she'd found it hard to focus on anything, when her imagination was so preoccupied with Bill Hamlin and his "business."

She came to the earth and shake hall and debated going in to try the "shake table," which simulated the feeling of an earthquake. She'd decided against it, thinking it made no sense to anticipate the worst. Anyway, she'd had a feeling that living with Bill Hamlin would cause her as much quaking as a woman could handle.

She didn't know how long she'd stood just inside the doorway, trying to decide whether or not to enter the hall, but when she went back around the corner to leave, she'd bumped right into the man from the motel in Mount View.

"Hello again!"

The man had acted as if he didn't know her. He'd seemed both shocked and embarrassed when she persisted.

"Don't you remember? The motel in Mount View. We met at the ice machine in the hall, and you asked me if I knew where—" She took a deep breath. "And by the elevator. You were already in it, and we were..."

"Yes. Yes." He'd almost run from her. She'd furrowed her brow as she watched him retreat, almost running down the hall.

And then she'd stood there, thinking, *Bill is going to find this one coincidence too many.*

But the more she thought about it, the more convinced she was that, except for the coincidence of having run into him again, there was nothing sinister about the man.

For one thing, he was way too attractive to be some kind of thug. And for another, both here and in the elevator of the motel, he'd seemed more frightened than frightening.

Still, she knew she should tell Bill, let him be the judge. But then, when he showed up with the car, she'd been so excited at starting the last leg of their journey that the meeting with the stranger had gone clean out of her head.

She'd given no further thought to the coincidence—until now. And now she knew that if she mentioned it, Bill would be furious with her for waiting so long.

"We'll stop up there at that café," Bill said, pointing over the steering wheel to his left, up ahead. "I'll bet you're hungry by now." The roadside café was lit up like a Christmas tree, beckoning to all the traffic trudging up the mountain.

"Oooh, that looks great!" Cara sat forward to get a better view of the place.

Bill glanced over at her and grinned. "You please easy, don't you?"

"I guess I do," Cara admitted. "But isn't that better than being a malcontent?"

"Who? You mean me?"

"Boy, you really are paranoid. No, I don't mean you, I mean in general."

Bill was in line behind another car, waiting for an opening to make a left-hand turn. He barely muttered his response.

Cara turned the sun visor down to look at herself in the mirror. She could use a bit of freshening up, she decided. A flash of red beyond her reflection caught her eye. She moved her head and saw a red car about two cars back. She was just about to fold the visor back in place, when she glimpsed a face on the passenger side of the red car that seemed familiar.

Was it the face of the bus driver who'd taken over when they left Mount View on the replacement bus?

"Bill?" She put her hand on his arm, but he was still concentrating on crossing the road.

"Hmm?"

"Bill, I think that's..."

"Damn!" Bill slammed on the brakes as the driver of a blue pickup changed his mind about letting him pass in front.

Cara grabbed the dashboard for support and then sat back with a shaky laugh when Bill turned to make sure she was all right.

"Sorry," Bill muttered. "I thought the guy was slowing to let me cross."

"It's okay," Cara said, pushing her hair back behind her ears.

Suddenly Bill grinned at her.

"What?"

"You look a lot younger today. Like a teenager."

"Is that a compliment?"

His grin hung on. "I don't know, that depends. What kind of a teenager were you?"

She gave him an impish grin. "Adorable."

He laughed softly, and their eyes clung for a moment. A moment in which they both suddenly found the interior of the car way too confining and their proximity far too stimulating.

The moment was interrupted by the blaring of a horn, and both of them looked up to see that a gray Datsun had come to a stop and the driver was gesturing for them to make the turn into the café's narrow parking lot.

The interior was as gaudy as the exterior, with highly varnished knotty-pine walls and booths that appeared almost gold. There were colored lights hanging from every surface, including the rafters.

Just as they were finishing lunch, Cara remembered the guy in the red car. She decided she'd been mistaken, that the man only looked like the bus driver. Replete with good food and Bill's surprising good humor, she decided it wasn't even worth mentioning.

It did occur to her that the coincidences were piling up, and that she was developing a habit of hiding things from Bill. But she promised herself that once they were settled in Santa Cruz, she was going to pay more attention and let Bill know if something made her suspicious.

THE SECOND-FLOOR furnished apartment they found was only two blocks from the Santa Cruz Beach Boardwalk, which meant plenty of foot traffic along their street. Bill felt a kind of security in the number of people who surrounded them as they went to and from their building.

The building itself was white stucco, a three-story structure with a flat roof where some of the tenants placed lounge chairs and sat out to catch the sun and the sea air.

Without discussion, Bill set Cara's gym bag in the larger of the two bedrooms, the one with a partial view of the pier and the ocean beyond. Cara thought it was a kindness at first, but then realized that Bill wanted the room that faced the front of the building and the street where "they" might appear.

Cara loved the apartment.

"Look, Bill, it's got a dumbwaiter. What do you suppose it's for?"

Bill came over and peered into the shaft. "Smells like they still use it to send garbage down to the basement. That used to be what these things were for in fancy apartment buildings."

Cara nodded and shut the doors. "You can tell this was one of those buildings. Did you see the concierge stand in the lobby?"

"Yeah. They had those things in the hotels in Paris when I—" He stopped in mid-sentence.

Cara put a hand on his arm as he started to walk away. "Go on, Bill. You were in Paris? When? What for?"

Bill pulled his arm from her grasp, as if her touch burned him. "Never mind, I don't have time to talk right now. We need groceries. Make a list and I'll go shopping."

"Wait a minute! I thought I'd go with you. It'll be fun."

Bill thought about it and then nodded. "Okay. But make your list first."

"I'm starving. Can we get some dinner before we go shopping?"

"I don't know." Bill shook his head and affected an exaggerated frown. "You've been eating an awful lot lately. How do you plan to keep that figure if you keep eating like that?"

Cara looked down at herself and then struck a pose. "Eating is how I keep this figure. You like?"

Bill pretended to study it for the first time. "It's okay."

Cara made a face and crossed her arms over one another. "Do you think I'm too fat?"

Bill laughed. "What are the criteria?"

"They say if you can pinch an inch, you're overweight."

"Hmm... Sounds like a plan." Bill started toward her, squinting, thumb and forefinger held an inch apart.

Cara stood her ground, waiting for his touch, wondering if she'd started something that could easily get out of hand.

Just as his hand came to rest on her waist, Cara shrank away, easing out of his grasp. "You're supposed to do it to yourself," she said with feigned harshness.

"We were talking about your figure," he retorted, his voice rich with controlled laughter.

Cara thought for a moment that, under different circumstances, Bill Hamlin would be a most delightful companion.

"Yeah, well, that's enough talk," she said with a sniff. "Let's make a list so we can get going."

They needed more than just food. Basically, they needed everything—cleaning supplies, paper products, linens and light bulbs.

Cara's mood grew morose as the list grew longer. Her share was going to use up all her funds. She'd have to find a job right away and hope her employer would pay weekly.

As if he'd read her mind, Bill broached the subject of money over the dinner they ordered at Antonio's, a little Italian restaurant about a block from their building. They were seated at a table off in a dark corner, with only a candle in a bottle for light. He was looking at the list she'd made.

"Listen, Cara, I have enough money to cover our start-up expenses. You might as well hang on to your money for now."

"No. We agreed to split everything down the middle," Cara said stubbornly. If she became too dependent on this man, he could pull the rug right out from under her anytime he felt like it. It would be *his* apartment, *his* food, *his* stuff. And she knew nothing about him. He might be one of those people who just changed his mind on a whim.

"Cara," he said softly, leaning across the table so that nobody else would hear. "You're going to need walking around money. You can't have much in that little gym bag of yours, and from the weight of it, I'd say you didn't bring a lot of the cosmetics and female stuff you women use. And what about clothes? If you're going to get a job to pay your share, you're going to need more than a couple of outfits, aren't you?"

She hadn't thought about all that. He was right. She didn't even have a change of shoes. It was becoming increasingly clear that she'd hadn't thought things out too well before she took off in the dead of night. There really was no reason why she couldn't have packed a real suitcase. It just went to show her state of mind at the time, and how terrified she'd been of anyone discovering her in the act of leaving and trying to stop her.

She sighed and bowed her head over her plate of spaghetti. "I'm just not comfortable with you taking care of me," she muttered.

Once again, his hand on hers sent more messages to different parts of her body than a friendly touch should.

His eyes had darkened to navy when she looked up into them.

"We agreed we were going to help one another, Cara. This is part of it. If you had the money, believe me, I wouldn't hesitate to take it."

"Perhaps your situation is more desperate than mine," she hinted.

"No 'perhaps' about it." He snatched his hand away and picked up his fork, returning his attention to his plate. "So look at it this way—you'll be earning anything I give you."

She grinned, relieved. "You need me," she said, strangely thrilled by the thought.

He wasn't as thrilled. His face darkened, and his hand, clenching his fork, whitened at the knuckles. "I don't need anyone! This was your idea, and I agree it's a good one. But don't think for a minute that I wouldn't have made it without you."

But then he saw the pain on her face. He put his fork down and sat back with a sigh.

"I'm sorry, Cara. I guess I'm both wired and tired. Forgive my bad mood."

"It's okay," Cara said softly. "We can pretend it's our first lovers' quarrel."

"I beg your pardon?"

Cara leaned forward and glanced from side to side, making sure no one could overhear them. "You know, like if we were really newlyweds, this could be our first quarrel."

With her face hovering in front of the candle, Cara was all softness and satin. Without thinking, Bill pushed the candle out of the way, while putting a hand behind her head to pull her nearer. "Now we can pretend we're making up," he whispered.

His grin was wicked before he leaned forward to brush his lips against hers. She tasted of marinara sauce and lip gloss. He let his tongue make another sweep, and this time she tasted like warm honey.

They clung together, their bodies slightly raised from their seats, for what seemed long moments, totally unaware of their surroundings. The sound of a tray crashing to the floor brought them out of their spell.

"Why did you do that?" Cara whispered, her lips still humming from the feel of his.

Bill shrugged, struggling to keep the grin on his face. "I told you, I was pretending it's our first time making up," he told her. But his voice was hoarse, and his own mouth ached for more contact with hers.

Cara nodded and returned to her food. Funny the way she'd felt so crushed when he said he didn't need her. She hadn't realized how important it was to her that she be important to him, to his sense of well-being.

"Good spaghetti," she said, her voice a bit unsteady. "But we'd better eat up if we're going to get groceries before the stores close."

It was at the supermarket that they learned their real differences.

Cara was excited to find a favorite brand of bologna in the cold-cuts case, while Bill ordered a pound of pâté from the deli case nearby. Cara grabbed frozen pizzas from the freezer section, while Bill stocked up on juice concentrates. Bill was ecstatic to learn that the market offered fresh fish, and Cara made a face at that and went to the snack aisle to find potato chips and honey-roasted peanuts.

They argued over brands—Bill preferring to read labels to determine ingredients, and Cara insisting the recognizable name was the way to decide the best buy.

"Did you eat like that growing up?" Bill asked, casting a dubious eye at a package of sweet rolls as he tossed his own choice—sesame bagels—into the basket.

"Nope. I ate like you do."

"So when did you decide that junk food was the way to go?" He poked gingerly at a cellophane-wrapped chicken-cheese burrito, that looked less like a burrito and more like a plastic model of chicken Kiev.

"In college. We weren't much into poached haddock in the dorm rooms. For one thing, we didn't have the facilities, and for another, we learned to just grab something easy that we could nuke in a minute and eat on the run."

"Well, we don't have a microwave, so you might want to put some of that stuff back, if that's the only way to prepare it."

They did agree on fruit, but Bill preferred apples and peaches and Cara chose the sweeter grapes and cherries.

Bill got a terrific surprise when they came to the meat counter and Cara and the butcher got into a knowledgeable discussion of the best way to prepare a pork roast.

"Where did you learn to make a pot roast?" Bill asked.

"My mom. She was a wonderful cook."

Bill halted in his tracks. "Was?" He hadn't told her about reading her journal. He knew he should, but the moment never seemed right. She wasn't going to take too kindly to learning he'd spied on her like that, read her most private thoughts.

"Is. She is a good cook." Cara busied herself reading a label on a can of sauerkraut. "Cabbage and vinegar," she muttered. "Go figure."

"Cara." Bill took her arm and gently pulled her away from the stack of sauerkraut. "Is it your mother you're hiding out from?"

Cara frowned and snatched her arm away. "I tell you what, Bill Hamlin. We'll trade. I'll tell you the story of my life and you tell me the story of yours."

They stared at each other over the wire cart of mismatched foods, and Bill knew they'd reached an emotional impasse. He realized, not for the first time, that they were barely more than strangers, traveling together through a haunted nightmare, each with his or her own secret to harbor. He could see in her eyes that Cara knew this, too.

She stayed ahead of him for the rest of the shopping trip, and when they came to the checkout she excused herself quietly and went out to the car to wait for him.

To Bill's relief—or at least that was what he told himself—they maintained an impersonal distance the rest of the evening, and only fatigue allowed them to fall instantly asleep in their separate rooms.

"CARA, WHERE ARE YOU?" Bill called out as he all but threw the grocery bag onto the kitchen table and went running through the apartment.

He stopped short and stared at her. She was on her knees beside the toilet.

"Are you sick?"

"Sick?" She stared up at him and then laughed, lifting her rubber-gloved hands up. "I'm cleaning the toilet."

Bill made a face. "Well, quit it. I got you a job. I mean, us. I got us both jobs."

"You got me a job? Really?" She was grinning and pulling the gloves off as she got to her feet. "Where? Doing what?"

"With me. At the boardwalk. The amusement park. You're going to sell ice-cream cones."

"Wow! Awesome!" She clapped her hands and did a little dance step. She stopped suddenly and leaned back against the sink, with a wry grin on her face. "Did you tell them I'm a college graduate with an M.B.A.?"

He stared at her, aghast. "Are you?"

"Yeah," she said with a nod.

"An M.B.A.?"

"You got it." She pulled the rubber band from her hair, releasing the ponytail to fall in a cascade of curls around her face.

"You're not old enough."

She turned to look at him, her chin thrust forward. "I'm twenty-six."

"When did you graduate?"

"Last month."

He sat down on the nearest seat, not even aware it was the toilet. "You just graduated, and you're on the run already?"

Cara shrugged. She looked into the mirror and fluffed her hair with her fingers. "What does one thing have to do with the other?" She didn't want to think about the fact that she'd met Douglas Harvard for the first time when he showed up at her graduation with her mother, their engagement already established, but news to her.

"It just seems sort of . . . sad."

Cara grimaced. Pity was not an emotion she desired to evoke in anyone, least of all Bill Hamlin. "Hah! You want to talk sad? What about your own situation?"

Bill's jaw tightened. "You really fight fire with fire, don't you?"

"Why shouldn't I? If you can dish it out, you can just learn to take it."

Bill laughed and got to his feet. "You're right. So do you mind if I say, I think it's too bad you haven't had a chance to use your degree yet?"

"What do you care?" she snapped, hurting and not quite understanding the reason.

"Because I know how fulfilling it is to do what you do best."

"Oh, yeah? And what is it you know so much about? What do you do best?"

"I was a C.P.A. before...before."

Cara's mouth fell open. "A C.P.—an accountant? That's bizarre."

Bill laughed. "Bizarre? Isn't that a little strong? I'm not exactly your garden-variety macho street punk, after all."

"No. But you were in the same field as me. Don't you find that...bizarre...or ludicrous?"

"You mean, too much of a coincidence?"

"Yeah, I guess I do."

"I don't believe in coincidence."

"Oh? Then how do you explain this?"

He couldn't. Was this a sign that they were really right for each other? Right for what? For holing up in a furnished apartment together, playing at marriage, playing at real life?

"I don't. I guess this is one of those times I'm wrong. Anyway, back to what I said originally—it's too bad you aren't going to be able to ply your trade."

Cara shrugged and marched out of the bathroom. "I suppose selling ice-cream cones could, technically, be considered running a business," she said over her shoulder.

"Yeah, well, you have to get over to the boardwalk and talk to the guy who has the ice-cream cart. He's holding the job until he talks to you."

Cara went into the kitchen and began putting away the groceries. "What did you do about all the vital statistics—like social security numbers, and so forth—and what are you going to be doing there?"

Bill cleared his throat. "I, ah...ahem...I have all that...all the papers and stuff, I mean. I'm going to be on the rides maintenance crew."

He tried to ignore her raised eyebrow, the questioning expression on her face.

"I can't use my social security number or my real name," she said.

"I told him you were my wife and that you hadn't ever worked before. He said he'd pay you in cash every week, that you'd be working for him rather than the park."

Now Cara cleared her throat, suddenly uncomfortable with this conversation. Somehow, Bill had papers that allowed him a real job on a real payroll, and yet he was on the run. How could that be? What made her most uncomfortable was that she couldn't ask. And how did he get a job as a mechanic? With those hands? No way. She shook her head, trying to clear away images and questions she didn't dare pursue.

"I'll go and change." She gave him a last look and left the room.

Bill sank onto a kitchen chair and stared at the clock on the wall over the sink without really seeing the time. How could this work, when these kinds of questions were constantly going to come up between them? Sooner or later she would demand answers, he was sure of that. She was already coming into focus as a lot more woman than he'd first suspected.

He shook his head, and took an apple out of the fruit bowl on the table, turning it over and over in his hands. An M.B.A. Not just a surprise there, but a hell of a co-incidence, considering his own business degree in conjunction with his degree in accounting.

He slouched back on his spine and began tossing the apple in his palm. If they were two people who'd met under normal circumstances, they'd have had quite a lot in common, actually. Hell, they could go into business together as a consulting and accounting firm. If they'd met any other way... at any other time... If he weren't who he was, and if he weren't on the run.

Forever.

He stood up and tossed the apple back into the bowl.

CARA LEFT a few minutes later, tucking her new light gray linen blouse into the waistline of her charcoal linen skirt.

Regardless of what Bill thought, she didn't really feel sad about her job. On the contrary, this was part of the adventure, the fun of it all. And she'd be out in the fresh air and sunshine every day, meeting people who were having fun and enjoying life.

For a moment, she let her mind open up to the memory of preparing to take her father's place in the family business—until she'd learned Doug Harvard had already taken over. But even if she didn't work for Dunlap

Industries, she was qualified to do better than sell ice cream for the rest of her life.

She blinked the thought away. Nothing was forever. For now, at least, she was going to make the best of things and accept what came her way. She was her own woman, her own person, and no meaningless job could take that away from her. Somehow, some way, she knew there was a fulfilling career in her future. This wasn't her future. This was now. And she was going to do her best to make it a happy time.

A big plus was the fact that she and Bill would be working together, seeing each other on the job, as well as at home. She wasn't prepared to examine her excitement about that too closely. Let it suffice that it was definitely a bonus.

Her step quickened and her pulse raced as she found more and more reasons to look forward to getting the job.

The crowd on the sidewalk around her was less dense than usual, but she didn't notice the man who crossed the street and kept her in his sights all the way to the boardwalk.

Chapter Five

It didn't take long to develop a routine. They started the day with a leisurely brunch, eaten at a table in front of the large window in the living room. The window was like a huge television screen with an ever-changing parade passing at all hours of the day and night.

Cara and Bill joined the throng around noon, after sharing the job of cleaning up after their meal.

At the pier, they would part, Bill going into the bumper-car concession, Cara moving down the same walkway to the ice-cream cart where Mr. Gambrini awaited her with a huge smile and a ready compliment.

"You look like rainbow ice cream today, Miss Cara," he might say, if she wore the multicolored blouse with the shawl collar, or "You are a chocolate-lover's delight, Miss Cara," if she wore the brown sundress with the little bolero jacket and woven raffia belt.

"You look pretty good yourself, Mr. Gambrini," Cara always replied, though she'd never seen the man in anything other than his white pants and jacket. He always had a clean white jacket ready for her to put on. That, along with a jaunty white cap, was her uniform.

Mr. Gambrini was old-world charming, and his good manners and warm welcome always made her start her workday with a smile. When he left her, he went on to oversee the food preparation for the evening meal at his family's restaurant, a few blocks from the beach. Periodically he would show up on a bike with a freezer unit on the back to make sure she had enough ice cream, or send one of his many nephews to give her a half-hour break. The nephews were less old-world, but just as charming, and all looked so alike she had no idea how many there were and which was which.

Sometimes, on her break, she'd wander around and watch people enjoying themselves on the rides or talk to the other concessionaires. Sometimes she'd go over to the bumper cars and chat with Bill, if he wasn't busy. When they spotted one another during the day, they'd wave and smile, and it made her feel as though they were really close, like best friends who shared everything. She looked forward to the evening meal, when they'd tell each other little stories about the day's happenings, people who stood out in their minds for one reason or another, or events that had made the day exciting or interesting.

When her shift was over, at eight, Mr. Gambrini, or one of those nephews, would return to take over for her. Bill finished at the same time and would be waiting in front of the bumper-car concession to walk her home.

They ate their dinner at one of the restaurants along the route home, since by the time they finished work it seemed too late to start cooking.

Mickey, their landlord, was the first one to inform them that they had a problem. He remarked to Bill that old Mrs. Jones on the first floor had pointed out that the Hamlins didn't seem much like newlyweds. Bill repeated Mickey's comments, and was obviously embarrassed by the telling.

"How the hell do newlyweds act?" he demanded, running his hands through his hair in a way that had become endearingly familiar to Cara.

The devilish imp in Cara raised its mischievous head and made a lewd suggestion, "Oh, you know," she said, as nonchalantly as possible, "more like they're in love."

Bill looked suspicious, bringing a laugh to the back of her throat. "What do you mean?"

She swallowed the laugh and kept a straight face. "Well, when we're out in public, I guess we should touch each other."

"Touch each other?" His voice went up an octave, and Cara looked away, hiding her face from his scrutiny.

"Yeah, you know. Like you should touch my hair, and I could rub your back a little, and you might pat me on the butt and I might caress your face." She reached for a glass and filled it with water from the tap. "Maybe we should stop and kiss now and then on the stairs, or when we're in front of the building or out back at the pool."

"Kiss?"

Hard to believe this guy was an educated, sophisticated man, the way he kept repeating her words, as if they were part of a foreign language.

"That's how married people act—especially newlyweds."

She swallowed some water before she risked turning to look at his face. It was flushed, and he was frowning. She almost felt sorry for him.

But in the following days she made a point of touching him when they were out in public, and, though he seemed a bit uncomfortable, he cooperated. If anyone observed them too closely, his reticence could be chalked up to shyness. After all, there were some people who weren't very comfortable about public displays of affection.

Cara's only problem was that it was becoming more and more natural to touch Bill—more something she wanted to do than just an act for the neighbors. Of course, she couldn't let him know it, but there were times when he played the role, and put his hand on her hair or touched her cheek, that she almost purred with pleasure.

Not only that, but sometimes his touch stayed with her for hours afterward, making her flesh hum as she went about her chores.

Even their disagreements felt like the kind of spats that happened between two people who really cared about each other, though they didn't have many of them.

At the beginning of the third week, they were having dinner at the Red Dragon Chinese Restaurant when they had one of those infrequent spats.

"It seems like the crowds get bigger every day," Cara said as she picked up big chunks of green pepper with her chopsticks.

Bill watched and shook his head in disgust. "Why do you order beef and peppers if you don't like the peppers?"

"I like the flavor," Cara said, shoving the pile of vegetables off to the side. She popped a piece of steak into her mouth and tucked it in the corner of her cheek before asking "Doesn't it?"

"Doesn't it what?"

"Seem like the crowds are getting bigger?"

Bill shrugged. "It's always the same to me—noisy, crowded, and busy."

It hadn't occurred to her that, like her, Bill was a fish out of water at his job. She longed to know what he'd done before he was forced to go on the run, but she knew she wasn't allowed.

She poked at her food. "I like to make the best of even the worst situation."

Bill grunted. "A job is a means of paying the rent. I don't see the need to glamorize it."

"Come on, Bill, this one's not your average humdrum job. There's the music, and people screaming on the roller coaster and laughing on the bumper cars. Having fun. There's the smell of the gyros frying and popcorn and cotton candy, and the ocean when the wind is up. There are all those people eating and drinking and running from ride to ride and to all the concessions, and..."

"And life is just a bowl of cherries, and laugh and the world laughs with you," Bill said, interrupting her, his tone tinged with sarcasm.

Cara made a face at him. "Okay, so I'm a little more optimistic than you are."

"A little?" Bill drank tea from a small blue-and-white bowl. "Sometimes I get the feeling life really is just a party for you, that this is all fun and games and not about the reality the rest of the world faces every day."

"Bill, is it such a crime to try to like your job? Your life?" Cara pushed at her food with her chopsticks, her appetite suddenly quashed.

Bill banged his fist on the table. Both Cara and the teapot jumped. "This isn't your life, Cara. This is what you have instead of your real life. This is make-believe. It could be snatched from you at any moment."

"By whom?"

He stared at her, plainly aghast. "Haven't I made it clear to you that I'm in trouble? That you're in danger if they find me and you're anywhere nearby?"

"Who, Bill?" All pretense of eating was forgotten. "Tell me who they are, who you're so afraid of. If they're a threat to me, too, don't I have a right to know?"

Bill swiped his hand across his mouth, then put it to his forehead, as if he'd suddenly discovered he had a headache.

Cara noticed that his once smooth hands were beginning to show the effects of his work. His palms had started to callus, and there were stains from machinery grease that didn't come off with plain soap and water.

"Bill?" she said, softly.

Bill slumped back in the booth and gave her a steady, noncommittal look. "Forget it, Cara. I'm not going to tell you anything. Nothing's changed. It won't help you to know any more than you do." He sat forward and dug in his pocket for his wallet. "Are you finished? Do you want a carryout box?"

As usual, his shutting her out made her feel numb. "Yes." She pulled her coin purse from her bag. "It's my turn, remember?"

"Oh, yeah." They were avoiding each other's eyes now, Cara realized, as uncomfortable with each other as strangers.

We are strangers, she reminded herself on the silent walk home.

The silence was all the more intense for the contrasting noise around them—people pushing by to get to the park for the last two hours of entertainment, or bumping tiredly along as they returned from the boardwalk.

At one point, someone stumbled against Cara, pushing her against Bill. He put his arm around her to keep her from falling—an automatic gesture that shouldn't have felt so personal, so caring.

And then, suddenly, it felt like more. She didn't know if it was his heartbeat or hers that thumped between them as she turned in his arms and was held tight against his chest. His mouth hovered temptingly close to hers, and she could smell his special fragrance, see the glint of desire that glowed in his eyes, feel his arms straining to hold her close. She wanted to slump against him, to let their bodies flow together, to quench the flame that burned the length of her body, from her thighs to her breasts.

Bill stared down into Cara's face. They were only a few feet from their own front door. He could scoop her up into his arms and carry her up to his room. He could see her as he lowered her to the bed, her eyes glowing with undisguised desire, as they were now. His hands ached to caress her silken skin, to curve around her breasts, to hold her against the heat of his own body.

Someone bumped against Bill's back, and he almost fell, taking Cara down with him.

He gritted his teeth and forced himself back to reality. He righted himself and loosened his hold on Cara. "Are you all right?" he asked.

Cara straightened and withdrew from his protective embrace. "I'm fine," she muttered. "Thanks."

"Good," Bill returned. His tone seemed surly to Cara. She wondered if they were going to go to bed in this same silence. She'd read somewhere that married couples should make up before going to bed—not let the anger carry over into the next day.

But we're not married, she firmly reminded herself. We're not really even a couple.

They arrived at their building. Cara tried the handle of the street door. "It's already locked for the night."

Bill handed Cara the bag containing their dinner remains while he fumbled for the right key. His head was bent, and Cara saw there was a swirl on top of his head where his hair curled into a cowlick. It made him seem more boyish, more accessible.

"Bill, let's make up before we go inside," some impulse moved her to say. She loved the apartment, didn't want it spoiled by bad feelings. Didn't want their closeness spoiled by bad feelings.

He found the right key and lifted his head so that now he was looking down at her. "Make up?"

"Yes, you know, stop being mad at one another."

She had her back to the door, and was facing him as she waited for him to unlock it. He studied her face in the dim light from the lamp over the door. "I'm not mad at you, Cara," he whispered.

She shook her head, as if to clear away a muddled thought. "I thought..." She cleared her throat, surprised to hear how hoarse she suddenly sounded.

"I get a little crazed on the subject of my mortality," Bill said. "I just don't want you to get so complacent you forget to be careful, is all."

Cara leaned against the door and wondered if it would prevent her fall, should her knees give way, as they threatened to do at any moment.

The kiss was fleeting—a mere suggestion of lips brushing. They stood apart, staring at one another.

Hunger flared in a brushfire of emotion. Cara felt her body slump against Bill's as his arms swept around to pull her to him—only the locked door kept them from falling.

Cara wasn't sure whether Bill pushed away first or whether she lurched free of his arms. The only thing she did know was that they were both breathing raggedly. She, herself, was wide-eyed with exhilaration mingled with fright.

"This isn't a show for the neighbors," Bill said softly.

Cara could only shake her head.

"We'd better get inside."

Bill put the key in the lock, and Cara followed him into the building, aware of a shakiness in the pit of her stomach.

Bill told himself he would not allow it to go beyond that one brief, out-of-control moment. She was delicious and available—a lethal combination for one in his predicament.

Cara told herself she mustn't forget their agreement.

She rushed toward the second floor, where privacy awaited them. Cara knew they were about to lose all control, to cast aside every good reason for keeping their relationship strictly platonic.

Bill reached the door of their apartment first. He stuck the key in the lock . . . and found the door unlocked.

THE MAN PUNCHED NUMBERS into the phone, reading them from a pocket-size notebook. It took five rings before the phone was answered.

"It's me. Lefebre," he said in response to a terse male greeting.

"It's about time! What the hell is taking so long?"

"I had to learn their routine, had to make sure I had time to do it."

"Is it done?"

"They don't have a phone."

"Come on! Everybody has a phone."

"Nope. No phone. But remember, they just moved in a few days ago. Maybe the phone company has a waiting list, or maybe they're in no hurry to order one because they don't know anyone here yet."

Frustration burned along the wires as the client sighed his disgust.

"So what did you find out?"

Lefebre was tempted to string the client along, which was a boost to his own ego—this feeling of power.

He relented, remembering the size of the fee he was charging for this assignment. Money had a power of its own. "They have separate bedrooms."

"What? Are you sure?"

"I'm pretty good at reading the signs. They're masquerading as husband and wife, but both bedrooms are being used. There's no crossover of clothing from one room to the other, no mingling of cosmetics or slippers or anything else to suggest either has ever stepped over the threshold into the other's room."

"Okay. Now listen. I want that phone bug in place the minute they get one installed. You got that?"

"Yes, certainly." His irritation was palpable. He resented a client treating him like an idiot. "And what do you want me to do in the meantime?"

"Keep to the plan. Try to find out all you can about the guy, and make sure they don't leave their present address without you knowing."

"You still want a regular check-in?"

There was a pause while the client thought that over. "Only if there's something important to report. I don't know if it's going to be necessary for me to come out there, but if it is, I need you to stay put, keeping them in your sights until then."

Lefebre hung up and lit a cigarette before leaving the shelter of the booth. From the street he could see the big window of the couple's apartment. There should be a light on pretty soon, he thought. They'd probably stopped for something to eat on the way home. It was what they'd done every night so far.

When the light came on, he could head back to the motel, a couple of blocks away. He moved across the street to his accustomed place in the doorway of a now defunct beauty shop. From his place in the shadows, he could see without being spotted from their second-story window across the street.

He worried that in his hurry to get out of their apartment he might have left some sign he'd been there. He probably hadn't. He was too much of a professional to make a mistake. And, after all, he hadn't even searched the place. The client had only ordered a phone bug, hadn't told him to toss the place, or to look for anything specific.

They were obviously underground. That was apparent, because he hadn't been able to find a thing on Hamlin's background so far. It was as if he'd just appeared out of thin air, making himself up as he went along.

Lefebre tossed the cigarette end and leaned against the wall. He was used to waiting, could actually doze on his feet like a horse and come instantly awake at the least sign of change anywhere in his vicinity.

Right now he needed to stay awake until the couple got in for the night. He passed the time by thinking about the client—a man with no name who was paying a hefty sum just to keep a surveillance going.

He'd been hired by phone. The call had come in the middle of the night.

"You'll have to leave right away. There's a flight out at 4:00 a.m. that'll get you to Utah before the bus gets there. You'll get on in Utah, and no one will question it. The bus is going to San Francisco and there'll be a rental car waiting for you there."

It had soon become clear that his quarry had become part of a couple. The two of them had taken all their meals together, as well as sharing a seat on the bus.

He'd thought he'd made a mistake when they separated in San Francisco, but then they'd joined up again in front of the Museum of Natural History.

Not for the first time, he wondered what the client was after. What was there about these people that his client would pay so much to keep tabs on them? The money had been deposited in his bank account, as promised. He'd made sure of that with a phone call to his bank the minute he got to Salt Lake. As he'd expected, the deposit had been made anonymously.

He was about to reach for another cigarette when the light went on in their apartment.

Good. They were in for the night. He could snatch a few hours of sleep before he went on with his research to discover what he could about Bill Hamlin.

BILL HELD CARA BACK with his arm and slowly opened the door. He jumped back, plastering himself against the wall, and waited. No sound came from within the apartment.

Cautiously he moved into the doorway, gesturing to Cara to stay where she was.

He turned on the front hall light and jumped back again. Still no sound, no movement. He eased over to his bedroom door and went through the same careful moves before entering his room. When he saw that the room was empty, he went to the closet. The briefcase was where he'd left it, pushed back against the wall, on the shelf. He took it down, unlocked it and removed the gun before continuing his search of the apartment.

Whoever had been there was gone. When he was sure of that, he went back to his room and pushed the gun between the mattress and the box spring. Only then did he call out to let Cara know it was safe.

"It's okay, Cara. Nobody's here."

Cara crept into the apartment on tiptoe, her eyes luminous with fear. "Are you sure?"

Bill met her in the little foyer and took her hands. They were icy, and he chafed them automatically. "Yeah, whoever was here is gone."

"Did they take anything?"

Bill laughed. "Like what?"

She looked surprised, but then smiled weakly. "Oh, yeah, you're right." Still, she moved with great caution down the central hall, as if someone might jump out at her. Bill had left lights on in every room.

"Who do you suppose it was?" she asked, inching forward to peer through the kitchen doorway.

"Probably a potential thief who was discouraged by the lack of salable items," Bill said. "I don't think he'll be back."

Cara nodded. "You're probably right." She pulled open a cabinet drawer and stared down at the odd assortment of unmatched flatware.

Bill went to her and looked over her shoulder. "Nothing missing, right?" he asked gently, with a half smile.

"What? Oh, right." She shut the drawer and looked around. Suddenly a chill swept over her, and she hugged herself for warmth. "It feels like such an invasion, anyway."

Bill agreed. "Still, when word gets out that we aren't worth the effort, I think the druggies and down-and-outers will strike us off their list of possible donors."

Cara gave Bill a searching look. "You're enjoying this," she said accusingly.

He couldn't tell her he was almost relieved that this had happened, that something had brought them back to reality after that mind-boggling kiss. If they hadn't found their apartment had been invaded, wouldn't they now be in bed, all caution thrown to the wind?

He shrugged and grinned. "I'm feeling a little smug, because our would-be burglar got zilch for his trouble."

The smile died on his lips as he suddenly realized he'd made a terrible mistake. He looked around, dumbfounded by his own idiocy.

"What's wrong with this picture?" he muttered.

"Bill...what's wrong?"

He ignored her as he stalked out of the kitchen and went from room to room, swearing under his breath.

A burglar would have trashed the place, would have hoped to find hidden bounty under or in other things. Most important, the intruder wouldn't have bypassed the locked briefcase—he or she would have assumed that the lock indicated treasure of some sort inside.

Suddenly the unlocked door seemed a sign of something far more ominous than a mere burglary. Bill went to the foyer and bent to examine the door lock more closely. No damage. The intruder had used a standard device, something as simple as a credit card. Bill hadn't thought to reinforce the lock, because he knew locks couldn't keep out the guys he was running from.

So this wasn't a thwarted burglary. But what, then? If it was Alvaretti's people, wouldn't they have waited and taken him out the minute he walked through the door?

"I'm going down to talk to Mick," he called out to Cara. "Lock up, and I'll be right back."

He could still hear her calling out questions as he ran down the flight of stairs and the long hall to the back of the building where Mickey, the landlord, lived.

Mick came to the door in a tattered corduroy robe, the sleeves short enough to expose the tattoos on his bare forearms.

"Honest, Hamlin, I didn't have no reason to go up to your place today," the caretaker said defensively when Bill questioned him. Bill was inclined to believe him, partly because he knew Mickey was too lazy to climb that flight of stairs even when there was a reason. When Bill and Cara had come to look at the apartment, Mick had just handed them the key and gestured toward the stairs. "Go on up and look it over. Let me know if you want it," he'd said. He'd never even asked if they'd locked up when they came back down.

"Did you see anyone around the place who doesn't live here?" Bill asked next.

"Naw. Same old same old. Most of you guys work over to the pier so I don't see you around during the day. Saw Mrs. Jones, of course. She don't go out much. Maybe she seen something or someone don't belong." Bill knew Mick spent more time watching the tube than he did taking care of the building or its tenants. It was likely the man hadn't been out all that day.

Mrs. Jones, according to Mickey, was a widow who had lived in the building before it became a residence for transients and seasonal workers. Most of the time she sat in her apartment on the first floor and watched people pass by her living room window, which was directly beneath Bill's.

"No, I didn't see anyone I haven't seen before," Mrs. Jones said in answer to Bill's inquiry. "You young people come and go so quickly these days, it's hard to keep up, but you know I have an excellent memory for faces.''

Bill decided to reserve judgment on whether or not she had such a good memory, but for now he had to accept her word. "No visitors out at the pool today?" he asked.

"Not today. Only people in the pool all day were 3B and 2C.''

He thanked her and went out into the hall, wondering if it was worth it to question anyone else in the building. But then he thought that would only draw attention to himself and to Cara and decided against it.

Maybe he was making too much of this in the first place. After all, it was just as likely that there'd been no intruder, that one of them had actually just forgotten to lock the door on their way out. He tried to recall which of them had been the last out, but for some reason all he could remember was their homecoming and their aborted lovemaking.

CARA LAY AWAKE for a long time that night.

At first, when Bill came back up from speaking to Mick, she'd expected him to say they would have to move. He hadn't however, and that had made her realize he didn't feel threatened. It had been a relief to see Bill without his usual paranoia ruling him.

Now, lying alone in the darkened room, she wondered if they would have made love if they hadn't found the door open. She'd never have admitted it aloud, but she knew she would have given herself to him with no hesitation. She had moved out of the realm of friendship in her feelings for Bill. Past the place of pretense. Past the point of weighing pros and cons. She'd out-and-out lusted after the man, and he could have had her right there on the front stoop if he'd wanted her.

Oh, yes, and he did want me, she thought. He may have changed his mind after the fact, but for a moment there, he was as hot for me as I was for him.

Just thinking about his heavy breathing, the way his eyes had glazed over, made her want him now. She turned on her side and willed the thought away. After some effort, she began to relax, began to drift toward nirvana. Her last thoughts were about the open door.

Bill had told her that he'd decided they hadn't really checked to make sure the lock was properly engaged when they left that day. She hadn't argued with him, because it had been such a relief to believe for the moment that they hadn't had an intruder.

But just as she was falling asleep, her memory returned to that morning, when they'd been leaving the apartment for work. She had been the last one out, and she had turned back and tried the knob, making sure the door had caught and was locked.

Chapter Six

The next day, Bill met her on her break and brought her bad news.

"They've asked me to work a different schedule, Cara," he said as they came to a park bench and sat down. "I'll be doing a split shift, coming in from ten till two and then coming back at six to work to closing."

Cara watched a family with small children settle on the grass to eat a picnic lunch as she digested what Bill had told her. "I guess that puts an end to our meals together."

"We could have breakfast together, if you wanted to eat a little earlier."

"I was just thinking that now most of the restaurants will be closed by the time you get off work."

Bill shrugged that off. "The only thing I'm worried about is you walking home alone every night."

"Why?" Suddenly the idea of entering the apartment alone at night loomed in her mind.

But Bill didn't refer to the previous day's episode. "There are a lot of nuts out there, Cara, people who mess with other people just for the fun of it. A woman alone, on the street, particularly at night... I'm just scared for you."

He sounded so truly worried that Cara's heart did a flip. Last night he'd shown his desire for her. Today he was showing concern for her welfare. The combination added up to something far more serious than mere friendship, in her estimation.

"I wouldn't be alone, Bill. There's always a whole parade of people from here to our street."

"And among that crowd could be a serial killer, or a drug-crazed mugger, or even a gang of teenage boys looking for a thrill at some woman's expense."

Cara shivered, despite the warmth of the day. "You really know how to put a girl's mind at ease, Hamlin."

"Cara, I'm scared to death that you're too much at ease. You need to keep in mind that we're fugitives, first of all, and secondly that you're a beautiful, sexy woman who's going to attract attention from all types of guys—perverts included!"

Beautiful. Sexy. They were his words, though he'd delivered them with a lashing tongue, with a frown on his face and eyes that glared angrily at her. She couldn't help but recall the night before, when those eyes had gazed helplessly, longingly, into hers.

She put a hand up to his face and caressed his soft beard. "It's sweet of you to worry about me, Bill, and I promise I'll be careful. But you have to work the hours they ask you to, and I have to walk home alone at night. There's nothing we can do about it."

He put his hand over hers, enjoying the feel of her palm against his face, holding it there a moment longer. "You could hang around here until closing, or I could tell them I have to leave at eight every night for fifteen minutes, just long enough to walk you home and come back."

Cara shook her head. "No. That's too much. You're always saying we shouldn't do anything to draw undue attention to ourselves. Wouldn't that make us stand out from all the other employees?"

Bill had to admit she was right. In order to develop and maintain anonymity, they needed to blend into the mass of boardwalk workers, as well as the community of ex-hippies, artists and tourists in their neighborhood. His first plan had been for them to move around a lot, but she had convinced him that settling down would make them seem less conspicuous and would tell the world they were just a normal married couple. And he was pretty sure she was right. If he had reservations, it was only because he stayed in his self-preservation mode at all times, regardless of the situation. Like last night. A false alarm, he was pretty sure, but he had to check it out, not take chances.

"Okay, but I want you to promise you'll keep your guard up when you go home at night."

"I promise, Daddy," Cara said, teasingly, yanking on his beard for emphasis.

Laughing, he slapped at her hand, tilting his head out of her reach. "Okay, you can make fun if you want, but just be sure you keep that promise."

Their breaks were over, and they headed back to their respective stations.

"By the way," Bill said just before they reached the bumper cars, "we're off on Sunday. Why don't we take the car and go exploring? We could go up into the mountains, to Felton, or maybe down to Carmel."

"Great! Oh, Bill, that's a wonderful idea. Thank you for suggesting it."

"Yeah, well…we need to drive the car once in a while, or the battery will go dead."

She thought about the pending trip on her way home, and about the way Bill had diminished the invitation by pretending his first thought had been for the car. It was almost as if Bill just couldn't stand to admit that anything in life was fun. Everything had to be so serious, so earnest. And yet she'd seen glimmers of humor—of teasing—in his personality, and the outing on Sunday had been his idea, something he'd obviously given some thought to.

Mr. Gambrini's nephew, Georgio, was her relief man this time, and she smiled and waved as she approached the ice-cream cart.

"Bella, Miss Cara," Georgio whispered, taking her hand and holding it to his chest for a moment.

"Talk about earnest," Cara said with a huge smile as she pulled her hand free.

"Beg pardon, Miss Cara?"

"Nothing. Forget it, Georgio." She pulled her hat from her jacket pocket and put it back on. She'd taken to doing her hair in a French braid, and the cap fit neatly atop that.

"See you at eight," she called out as the young man strutted off into the crowd.

A group of teenagers came up just then, and it took a long time to fill their orders, what with the way they kept changing their minds about which flavors they wanted. There was one moment, as she waited, ice-cream scoop poised between rocky road and bubblegum, when she looked up and saw a man standing across the boardwalk, staring at her, and her pulse quickened in her chest. Was it the man from Mount View and the museum in San Francisco? She couldn't be sure, because of the sunglasses. But when she'd filled the cone and looked up

again, the man wasn't there. She didn't think of him
again until she started her walk home alone that night.

It was still light out, and, as she'd pointed out to Bill
earlier, there were plenty of people coming and going
around her.

But she was used to a leisurely stroll beside Bill, their
arms often brushing, his hand sometimes grabbing her
elbow to keep her steady when someone bumped into
them. She hadn't realized how much she'd miss that.

Tonight she seemed to be pushed along by the moving
throng, almost battered in the turmoil of people hurrying to enjoy the last couple of hours of entertainment at
the pier, or rushing to get back to their cars or homes after a tiring afternoon at the park. She wanted to stand
still, balking, refusing to move another inch at any pace
but her own. But if she did that, she'd make a fool of
herself at best, and be trampled underfoot at worst.

She saw the man again, just a few feet ahead of her,
keeping pace with the crowd, his head towering inches
above those on either side of him. She was sure it was the
same man, because of his height, his thick blond hair,
and the dark shirt he wore.

Chilled air seemed to spiral down the back of her neck,
but then it occurred to her that the man was ahead of her,
not following her, so he couldn't be someone she should
fear. Hanging out with Bill was definitely having an adverse affect on her.

That was when she remembered another word Bill had
used that day. *Fugitives.* "We're fugitives," he'd said.

She put the word into a familiar context in her mind.

Fugitives from the law.

She stopped in her tracks, unmindful now of the people around her, unmindful of the people who brushed
past her and against her, until one almost knocked her

down. She moved off the sidewalk, ducking into the nearest doorway. It was the Italian restaurant where they'd had dinner their first night in Santa Cruz.

The place was fairly busy at this hour, but she found a small table set against the back wall and fell onto a chair as her mind spun in an eddy of remembered phrases, recalled images.

The waiter called out something as he passed by with a laden tray at his shoulder. The words didn't penetrate Cara's consciousness.

If Bill was a fugitive from the law, didn't that mean he was one of the very same bad guys he'd warned her about when he was cautioning her about walking home alone? For all she knew, he could be an escaped convict, a bank robber on the run, a rapist... Her mind flashed to the intensity of his embrace the night before. What if they hadn't been out in the open when he kissed her, what if she'd refused to go any further. Would Bill have refused to take no for an answer? His arms had been so strong, so tight around her. Would she have been able to escape them if he was determined to hold her against her will?

A gasp of anguished fear filled her throat, caught on a ragged breath, turned into a harshly burning cough. The waiter came running up with a glass of water, shoving it at her, patting her on the back.

She took a swallow, choked, pushed away. "Th-thanks." She coughed again, swallowed again, cleared her throat and smiled through her tears. "I'm f-fine, really," she insisted. She wiped her eyes with the palms of her hands, and when she lowered her hands, she realized the other diners were all looking over at her with concern.

She snatched up a menu and pretended to read it, keeping her face hidden until she was sure the other patrons had turned back to their own business.

LEFEBRE LIFTED HIS HAND and looked into the small mirror cupped in his palm. Moving it back and forth, he studied the reflections of faces over his shoulder, looking for the girl. Gone.

He spun around and searched the crowd, people pushing past him, some muttering angrily that he was in the way. Obviously, Cara had made a stop in the last block and a half. He moved to his right and joined the group moving back toward the pier.

When he came to the Italian restaurant, he peered in through the windows. He didn't see her at first. She was all the way at the back of the room, near the kitchen doors.

Should he take a chance on her recognizing him, or wait outside? And what about Hamlin? Where was he? Cara'd stopped at the bumper cars as usual, but then gone on alone after waving at someone, ostensibly her pseudohusband. He'd been alternating his tracking of the couple, some days following Hamlin, some days Cara Davis. His decision to follow her, rather than wait and follow Hamlin had been based on something other than professional wisdom. He couldn't remember exactly when she'd begun to occupy so many of his thoughts. Had it been when he stood in the doorway of her bedroom, after studying Hamlin's room, and realized it had the pristine quality of a place where a woman slept alone? Or had it been the day at the boardwalk, when he watched her kneel and lift the hem of her dress to wipe the eyes of a crying child who had apparently become separated from its parents? He'd had a good view of a long, smooth thigh, right up to that place where hip meets panty in a beckoning curve toward one of the most vulnerable parts of a woman's body, and he'd felt the telltale clamoring in the pit of his stomach.

She was a movable feast of color and style, her reddish gold hair worn differently most days, her clothing brightly patterned, her skin, almost alabaster the first day he'd seen her, now tawny from the California sunshine.

Now, when he stood across from their building and watched the light go on in their apartment, he felt a twinge of envy that Hamlin got to close himself in with her for the night while he, Lefebre, had to return to a lonely motel room. He was beginning to hate Hamlin, even though he knew the couple weren't having sex. He'd been watching for the signs, and they hadn't changed. Oh, sure, they'd started touching more, paying more attention to one another, but that could be part of the act of pretending to be married.

That should have made him feel better, but now it was like waiting for the other shoe to drop, because he couldn't believe that Hamlin wasn't going to go after the girl sooner or later. The guy wasn't a eunuch, was he?

He decided not to enter the restaurant, not to take any more chances. Today she'd looked up right into his eyes when she spotted him across the boardwalk. He'd seen the reaction. Fear. Not one of recognition, however, which told him she'd just been frightened by the fact that she'd caught a stranger staring at her. With good reason, he knew. People on the run became paranoid after a while, trusting no one, fearing everyone.

He moved away from the window, jaywalking across the street, in front of a cab whose horn blared an angry warning at him.

If she was going to have dinner there, he had time to call his client. The man had insisted that he make the calls from different phones each time, always using a public phone. Personally, he thought his client was just as paranoid as the couple, but he didn't question it, merely did as he was told—at least most of the time. No skin off his nose. Twice he'd ignored the client's orders and called from the motel, putting the call on his credit card, figuring the client would never know the difference, but for the most part...

The ringing stopped, and a man answered. Lefebre made his report.

"No phone yet. I've waited every day in front of the building, and no phone company truck has shown up"

"They're still in the same place, still at the same jobs?"

"Yep. Doesn't look like they're on the move. Looks like they're in it for the long haul. You should be able to zero in on them anytime you want." He hesitated. "So...uh...you want me to back off now?" He hoped the client couldn't hear the slight edge of pleading in his voice, couldn't recognize that Gordon Lefebre was getting hooked on this one. He knew that happened sometimes in his line of work. Becoming enamored of the prey. Not always sexual interest. Sometimes you got to watching a guy and your curiosity got piqued to the point where you had to know what happened next, couldn't stand to leave in the middle of a scenario. Once he'd done surveillance on a woman and her lover for the woman's husband. Their lovemaking had been so exquisite that he couldn't stand to miss a moment of it. He'd continued to watch every day for a week after he'd reported his findings to the husband. That was how he'd happened to be watching when the husband burst into the room and shot the lovers. Lefebre had never quite recovered from that, from feeling as if he'd caused the murders.

He hadn't turned himself in as a witness, and his conscience didn't bother him on that score, but after that he'd refused to take any more errant-spouse jobs.

"Hell, no!" the man shouted, bringing Lefebre out of his reverie. He held the receiver away from his ear for a minute and then put it back in place. A relieved grin lit his face, giving it a puckish look.

The client went on, "The object is for you to stay with them until I can get out there myself. What if they decide to move in the meantime?"

"Yes, right, I get it." Lefebre quit smiling, almost afraid the client would hear the happiness in his voice. "Listen, how long before you think you'll get out here?"

"I don't know.... That isn't your concern, anyway."

"It's just I was looking forward to meeting you in person," Lefebre said.

A mirthless chuckle came down the wire. "That's not going to happen, Lefebre. You'll be told to leave twenty-four hours before I arrive, and I expect you to follow orders." The client's tone grew ominous as he added, "If you know what's good for you."

Lefebre wasn't afraid of anyone. But something in the client's voice caused a chill to run up his back. Not for the first time, he wondered what the client had in mind for the couple, what their connection to him was.

BILL WAS TIRED AND HUNGRY when he got home that night. It had been a long day, and he hadn't been able to get up the energy to stop at a restaurant for dinner. This would have been a good night to come home to a meal prepared by Cara, but he didn't expect it and wouldn't ask her.

He was rummaging around in the fridge, looking for something filling, when Cara came to the kitchen door.

He lifted his head and gave her a tired smile. "I see you got home without incident."

"I'm fine. There's a carryout of spaghetti in there, if you're hungry. I didn't touch it."

Bill found the box and then looked up at her when he opened it and found a full portion. "Did you get this for me?"

"No..." She shook her head, averting her eyes. "I ordered it and then found I really wasn't hungry, so I had them box it up."

He held it out to her. "Won't you want it later? Or would you like to share it now?"

"No. You eat it." She turned and went out of the room.

"Hey," he mumbled to himself, "was it something I said?"

He'd never really seen her in a bad mood. "Peckish," his grandmother would have called it. It was the way his grandfather got when dinner was late. But Cara had said she wasn't hungry. He didn't know what to do. He wasn't inclined to go after her. After last night, he'd made a pact with himself that he was going to keep a greater distance between them. That was one of the reasons why, when his boss asked if any of the guys wanted to work the split, he'd jumped at the chance. It was true he didn't like her walking home alone but, all in all, she was probably safer on the street than alone with him. This way, they wouldn't be thrown together all the time, and temptation wouldn't get a chance to rule him.

So whatever was bothering her now, she'd have to get over it herself.

He dumped the pasta into a saucepan and adjusted the gas to let it simmer before he sat down at the kitchen table and unfolded the newspaper. Determined as he was to keep his distance, he found that he couldn't focus on the paper, that he kept lifting his head to listen for her movements in the other room.

The apartment seemed strangely silent after the continual noise of the day, especially now that Cara wasn't in here chatting with him. "I'll get a TV set," he grumbled. "And maybe even a stereo."

He'd warned Cara that they might have to leave their current address at a moment's notice and, for that reason, he didn't want to be tied down by material things. She'd agreed, insisting she'd like a life without television, radio and sundry mechanical gadgets. Now he thought maybe just a small TV wouldn't be so bad. Just a small black-and-white screen—something he wouldn't regret leaving behind if they did have to run.

They.

Would he still take her along if his whereabouts were discovered by Alvaretti's people? It wouldn't make much sense. It would mean they knew he was traveling with her.

No, if he was made by the wise guys, he'd have to go on alone, leaving her to find a different life for herself.

He tried to visualize what that life might be. She wouldn't have to run forever. After all, that Harvard guy might be a world-class jerk, but he was no real threat to Cara. She could always tell her mother the truth. The woman's feelings would be hurt, but she'd actually be better off knowing the truth. Maybe he should talk to Cara about that, advise her to come clean with her mother. It would mean confessing that he'd read her journal, but maybe that, too, would be in Cara's best interest.

He could imagine her talking to her mother on the telephone at the drugstore down the block—the tears of relief, the promise to be home soon. He'd probably drive her up to San Francisco, to the airport.

And then he'd come back here to this apartment. Alone.

The spaghetti sauce burped loudly, on the verge of burning. Bill prepared his plate, then sat down to eat.

It dawned on him, as he raised the first forkful to his mouth, that this was the first meal he'd eaten alone since he'd met her, except for that one time during the bus trip when she'd had a headache.

He got up and went to her room. The door was closed, and he knocked gently.

"Yes?"

"It's me." Sap! he told himself. Who else would it be? He rubbed his fingertips in a circle along the wood grain of the door. "Are you feeling all right? Can I get you anything?"

"No. I'll be fine. I just want to be alone." Her voice sounded weak, faraway.

"Oh ... well ... if you need anything ..."

"Thanks."

He stood there a moment longer, nervous and uncertain. Should he press the issue, insist she open the door so that he could see for himself that she was all right? But what if it was a woman thing, and she really just wanted to be left alone? He didn't know much about these things.

If she's really sick, she'll let me know, he assured himself, and went back to his solitary meal.

CARA PRESSED her palms to her eyes and shook her head as she listened to Bill's receding footsteps. She couldn't hole up in this room every time Bill was home, hiding from whatever threat he might pose. And furthermore, there hadn't been any sign of malice in his voice when he offered his help. For that matter, she'd never really seen anything in Bill Hamlin's nature to indicate that he meant her any harm. Well, at least not after that one time when he'd tied her to the chair in her motel room.

She'd thought then that he was a sexual deviant, and he'd proved her wrong. Certainly, if he was a rapist or a killer, he'd have taken advantage of her then. And hadn't he come back to untie her, not knowing she'd gotten out of the bindings herself? Was that the act of a criminal?

But even criminals had soft spots for some people in their lives. Their mothers, children, wives—even their dogs. Okay, so assuming the worst—that Bill Hamlin was a fugitive from the law—that didn't mean he would hurt her. She'd been safe with him so far. They'd slept under the same roof for almost a month now, and he'd never come anywhere near her bedroom door until just now.

She began to feel foolish. Once again she'd let her imagination carry her far astray from reality. She sat up on the edge of the bed, her chin in her hands, and tried to decide what she should do.

The obvious thing, if she was in doubt, was to go to the police. She pulled up a mental picture of Bill in jail, behind bars. The thought was dreadful. She jumped up and began to pace the room. She'd seen enough cop movies to guess that if the law was really after Bill, she could be considered an accessory or, at the very least, guilty of harboring a criminal.

She stopped at her window and looked out. Her room was on the south side of the building, looking out over the pool. At times she liked to sit in the dark and look down on the blue water, lit from below by pool lamps.

Sometimes a lone swimmer would do laps, and sometimes a couple would come out and swim slowly, seductively, around one another, splashing water and then stroking away sensuously. She wasn't much of a swimmer herself—in fact, she'd yet to even try on the new suit she'd purchased their second day here. Bill, on the other hand, used the pool at least once a day.

As if she'd conjured him from her thoughts, Bill suddenly appeared on the deck below her window, one of their striped towels slung around his neck, his body bare except for the brief black trunks he wore. He went to the edge of the pool, tossed the towel onto a nearby lounge chair and dived into the water without ceremony.

Cara gasped softly, amazed by the beauty of his body and form. He was attractive in clothing, but half-naked, using his body athletically, he was a work of art. She pressed closer to the window, not wanting to miss a single stroke as Bill did smooth, rapid laps from one end of the pool to the other, over and over. The water barely rippled around him as he moved his arms in and out, lifting his head every other stroke to take in air. She knew nothing about the sport, but she guessed he was probably good enough for competition.

When he lifted himself from the water, he did it with the same unhurried ease with which he'd dived in, using his arms to pull himself up onto the deck.

Cara's gaze never wavered as she watched Bill bend to retrieve the towel and dry his face, his hair, and then his body.

She realized that she was actually spying on him, that he might be uncomfortable if he knew she was watching his every move. But she couldn't stop, couldn't tear her eyes away from the sight of all that masculine beauty.

He stood a moment, staring down into the water, and then he put the towel back around his shoulders and moved away from the pool, back into the building and out of her view.

Cara crept back to her bed and lay down on her side, her breathing shallow, though her heart seemed to be pumping at top speed.

Bill Hamlin was probably wanted by the police in half the country, judging by the way he protected his identity, and she should probably be scared to death of him. But one thing she knew for sure—if he came into her room right now, his body still cool and damp from his swim, his hair curling around his ears in wet ringlets, his skin glistening, his muscles defined by his every movement, she would open her arms to him and hold him forever safe from whatever demons were chasing him.

Chapter Seven

The next day, Cara was her usual sunny self, pushing Bill away from the stove to scramble his eggs herself, jokingly putting an apron around his neck like a bib when he sat down to eat in his clean work clothes.

When he left for work, Bill turned back and said, "Don't forget we have a date on Sunday."

She wouldn't forget. It loomed large in her mind for most of her waking hours. Her fantasies brought a smile to her lips, a fever to her skin.

It was hard getting used to Bill's new schedule. She knew she was going to be lonely in the days to come. She thought it would be wise to start cultivating friendships among her neighbors and her co-workers.

But for now, she had Sunday to dwell on, to look forward to. It was three days away and by the time it rolled around she could hardly contain her excitement.

They drove up route 9, into the Santa Cruz Mountains, joining a long line of traffic made up of tourists and Sunday travelers like themselves. Cara could see how the early Californians had sculpted the mountain to create homes and businesses. The inside, along the mountain itself, seemed safe and inviting. But on the outside of the mountain there would be a patch of trees, or even a driveway leading into a property, and then suddenly the land would fall away in a sheer drop that made Cara nervously lean in toward Bill.

"I didn't know you were afraid of heights," Bill commented, obviously sensitive to her discomfort.

"I didn't think I was. But for some reason this feels so open, and the openness feels like it could just suck us right into it, right over the edge."

Bill laughed at her imaginative description. "Don't worry, love, I'll grab you if it looks like an alien is about to snatch you out of the car and over the edge."

Cara made a face at him and gingerly moved back to her own side of the seat.

"Speaking of heights, would you like to see the redwoods?"

"Oh, yes!" All fear of the mountain was forgotten, and in moments Bill was turning the car into the Henry Cowell Redwoods State Park. The fact that it was on the outside of the mountain never even occurred to Cara, so excited was she by the sight of the sequoias, some of them thirty feet in diameter, with their trunks extending skyward for what looked like miles.

Their size created a feeling of shelter in the park, and as they walked along the paths, with patches of sunshine falling on them between the trees, Cara had a feeling much like that of being in a church. The feeling seemed to be universal, for Cara noticed that all around her people were speaking in hushed tones, and that everyone in the park had the same look of awe on their faces.

She glanced over at Bill and saw that he, too, was affected by the grandeur of the big trees.

As they walked along, Cara stumbled on a root embedded in the path, and Bill reached for her hand to steady her. Without thinking about it, they continued to hold hands as they strolled deeper into the forest.

They came to a park bench and sat down to enjoy the mystique of the park and the trees. Their hands separated, but the good feeling of camaraderie continued.

"This is heaven," Cara whispered, her voice quivering with happiness. "I don't think I can bear to leave it."

"Yep. I'm sure this is exactly what heaven is like," Bill said, gazing skyward. "But have you noticed, nobody's set up camp here?"

"What do you mean?"

Bill shrugged. "I think people don't want too much of a good thing. I think they like the idea it's here and they can come back over and over and find it here, but they don't want to stop their normal lives and move in here."

"I would."

He glanced down at her and saw that her face was etched with reverence.

"Yeah. Well, you'd get tired of it soon enough, especially when you found out they don't make pizza deliveries into the park."

"Oh, you!" Cara punched Bill's arm and moved a few inches away from him. "You are absolutely the most cynical person I've ever met in my life."

"And you've met tons of cynics, right?"

Cara sniffed and looked away. "None like you, you can be sure."

Bill laughed, the sound drifting away in the acoustical vacuum caused by the trees. "Cynicism may be a misnomer, my dear. Perhaps I'm just more realistic, more pedantic, better educated in the ways of humankind, than most people."

Cara studied him a moment and then said, "Perhaps the only reason you don't see anyone camped out here is because it's against park rules."

Bill stared back at her and then grinned. "Touché."

They were quiet for a while after that, each privately celebrating the beauty around them. By the time they started back down the mountain, they were both tired and sated with the beauty of it all. On the drive down, it was the passenger side that was on the inside of the mountain, and Cara was able to lean back and enjoy the ride in drowsy contentment.

It was easy to forget the past, forget any future threat, forget they were only playing at being a couple. It had been a perfect day—a day that promised to end with a perfect night, Cara thought. The weather was balmy, and by the time they reached Water Street, she was not surprised to find the town teeming with both tourists and locals enjoying the early-evening warmth.

As they turned into their street, they could see that some of their building's tenants were enjoying the weather on the roof of the building. Cara recognized the couple from 3B, and the three college women who shared the apartment on the first floor, across from the laundry room.

She touched Bill's arm, meaning to draw his attention to the sight, when suddenly the air was rent by the most horrendous noise she'd ever heard. In an instant, the building was engulfed in flames, and the people on the roof went flying in all directions.

Later, Cara didn't remember Bill stopping the car or exactly when they had decided to get out. But all at once they were in the street, with people screaming and running in panic around them.

A man's voice yelled, "What was it, an earthquake?"

Someone else called out, "No, it was an explosion...like some kind of bomb!"

Bill grabbed Cara's hand and began to pull her down the street.

"Wait...wait, Bill! Don't!" She tried to pull free, desperately needing to know what had caused the explosion, what was happening to the building she'd come to think of as home, even though they'd lived there only a few weeks.

"It's going to be a media circus here any minute, Cara," Bill growled through clenched teeth. "Come on!"

They left the car where it was. Cara wondered why but couldn't draw enough breath to ask. She was gently but firmly pulled through the streets of Santa Cruz, until Bill stopped in front of a small bar on a side street and jerked her inside. The lettering on the window decreed it the Backstreet Bar and Grill.

She was still out of breath moments later, when a laconic bartender put down the daily-newspaper crossword puzzle and asked for their drink order.

"Give us a couple of brandies," Bill panted, and then added, "No ice, and make 'em doubles."

"Been running?" the bartender asked as he reached for two glasses.

"Yeah," Bill said, turning to study the layout of the place. There was a door marked Exit at the back. Probably led to an alley. Good, Bill thought. There were doors marked Gents and Ladies, and another, with a round glass window, that obviously led to a kitchen. For the moment, they were the only customers in the place, and it didn't appear that anyone was in the kitchen to give credence to the "Grill" part of the title on the window.

The bartender squinted at each of them in turn. "Not dressed for running," he commented, in that same monotone.

Bill spun around, glaring at the man, and then decided the guy was not suspicious, but merely making bartender conversation. He forced calm into his voice and manner. "No. We decided to take a run after we were already out and about."

The barman poured an estimated double in each glass and pushed the drinks toward them.

"Six bucks," he said.

Bill paid for the drinks, adding a two-dollar tip, and led Cara to a table in the far corner, near the back door.

It wasn't until they were seated, and Bill held the glass to her lips, that Cara began shaking. Her teeth chattered so badly that the liquor spilled down her chin.

"Swallow it, baby," Bill ordered, his voice a harsh whisper.

She nodded obediently and tried another swallow. This time some of the brandy went down her throat. Warming. No, burning. And then tickling harshly. She began to cough, and Bill jumped up and went to the bar.

The bartender already had a glass of water poured and held it out to Bill. "Thanks," Bill muttered, and moved swiftly back to Cara, who held her hands to her face and was still coughing. Bill could see that her hands were trembling.

She took the glass and gulped the water thirstily, tears spilling down her cheeks.

Bill prayed the tears were the result of the coughing spell, but knew they were probably tears of emotion and delayed shock, as were the shaking and the chattering teeth.

He rubbed her back and urged another drink past her quivering lips.

"I'm...I'm okay," she said finally, clenching her fists in her lap and refusing any more liquor.

Only then did Bill drink his own, taking it all in one continuous swallow. He grimaced, shook his head and growled low in his throat. It was the only sign that he was unaccustomed to strong drink.

"Why did we have to run away?" Cara demanded in a harsh whisper. "Maybe we could have..." She began to cry. "Maybe we c-could have h-helped," she stammered.

Bill gestured for the bartender to pour another round before he answered Cara.

"What if that explosion wasn't an accident?" He leaned toward her and whispered the question so softly that she could barely make out the words. She could feel the warmth of his breath, though, and smell the rich aroma of the brandy.

"Wh-why..." She shook her head, tried to assimilate the idea, shook her head again. "No!" The horror of the thought actually stopped her crying.

Bill squeezed her hand, warning her to keep quiet as the bartender approached the table with another round of drinks. They exchanged drinks for money. Bill handed him an extra bill. "How about one of your cigarettes?" he asked, nodding toward the man's shirt pocket, where a cigarette pack bulged.

The barman looked at the denomination of the bill and left the half pack with Bill. It wasn't until Bill lit one, inhaling a deep, harsh mouthful of smoke, that Cara reacted.

"You don't smoke."

"Used to," Bill said, pulling deeply at the filter. "And at least for today, I do again." The first drag made him cough briefly, but he took a second just the same, enjoying the immediate comfort it gave.

"Tell me why you think..." She rubbed the vestiges of tears from her cheeks with her palms.

Bill took another drag, exhaled, and set the cigarette on the lip of the metal ashtray, satisfied just to have it ready at hand. "I just think it's a possibility. I don't like coincidences."

"Coincidences? Such as?"

"Such as finding our door unlocked the other night. By itself? Nothing. Coupled with the explosion? Suspicious." He shook his head. "Coincidences? I don't think so."

He sipped his drink and lifted the cigarette from the ashtray, almost surprised to find it there. He inhaled and grimaced satisfaction.

Cara glared at him and nodded toward the cigarette. "Why would anyone need to use a bomb to kill you? They could just wait for you to develop lung cancer."

Bill's face twisted in a wry smile at the absurdity. Was she really worried about the state of his lungs at a time like this? "Uh-uh. That'd take too long. Anyway, it took an explosion to drive me back to smoking, didn't it?"

"How are we— Oh, Bill, what does this mean?" She started to cry again.

This time Bill took her into his embrace, holding her head against his chest, and let her cry.

When her sobs quieted enough that she could hear him, he told her what they were going to do.

"We'll wait to hear the police and fire department reports. If I'm just being overly suspicious and it really was an accident, we'll get another apartment, new clothes, and go back to our jobs."

"And if it wasn't an accident?" Caramel highlights in her brown eyes coupled with the alarm in her voice to define her terror.

How did he explain that he'd have to leave her? Wouldn't she feel totally abandoned after such a horrendous shock?

He shook his head. "We'll decide that when the time comes. Sip your drink, Cara, it'll make you feel better. I'm going back to get the car, and then I'll come back for you and we'll go to a hotel for the night. We can keep abreast of the news on the TV."

Retrieving the car was most important. After finding the door to the apartment unlocked, Bill had decided to take no chances—he'd moved his briefcase to the trunk of the car, further hiding it by placing it beneath the spare tire. It contained his nest egg, alternative identities, and a loaded pistol. It was all that was left of Bill Spencer.

"JEE-ZUS!" Lefebre said into the phone. "You should see the mess. One whole side of the building just caved in on itself."

His client's excitement was palpable. "They were killed?"

"Nah. They weren't even there. I mean, they weren't in the building. They drove up just as the building went. Then they just disappeared."

"Disappeared?" The man's voice went up an octave. "You mean you lost them!" he shrieked.

"Hey, wait a minute, Bub. Given the circumstances, I think you should cut me some slack. A building just exploded, and several people were most likely killed. In the midst of all that, I should think you'd figure I might have taken my eyes off them for a minute. I followed them all day, after all. Went clear to the top of a mountain, for Pete's sake. I had to keep a good distance, so I spent most of the day with my eyes glued to binoculars and nothing to eat, 'cause I didn't know how long they'd stay in any one place. At that point, I had a headache, I was hungry and tired, and I pulled up a couple of car lengths behind them and their building goes boom! Yeah, I lost 'em, and so would have you.''

"Okay, okay. Calm down. Now listen, I know it won't be easy, but get on it right away. Santa Cruz isn't that big. Find them. Now.''

"Yeah, sure. I'll get on it right away, boss. You bet.''

Lefebre hung up and swore under his breath. He still hadn't gotten over the shock of it. Part of a building going up like that. Jee-zus! What if they'd been in the building at the time? What if the girl had been killed? What a waste that would have been, a beautiful girl like that. Young, lush, gorgeous. Had it been only his imagination, or had the client sounded like he hoped the couple had been killed?

He stared at the phone. Cold-blooded bastard. Well, he had another thing coming if he thought Gordo was going to do another thing before he got some aspirin, some food and some rest—in that order. The client was right about one thing. Santa Cruz was a small city. He'd find them again soon enough—even if soon enough meant tomorrow.

CARA EMPTIED one of the packets of hotel-supplied bubble bath into the stream of hot water. She lay back in the rich lather and let the heat, the steam and the fragrant emollients permeate her skin. She felt cold right to the core of her being, felt as if she'd never be warm inside again. She slid lower into the water, submerging herself all the way to her chin.

She drifted in and out of consciousness as hot water and fatigue drained her. The brandy had begun to kick in, and she felt slightly buzzed. A gentle tap at the door barely roused her.

"Yes, Bill," she called out, in a sleepy singsong.

"I've got a hot drink for you, Cara."

"Mmm . . . Okay, Bill." She kept her eyes closed, unconcerned about Bill coming into the bathroom, knowing she was covered by the soap bubbles.

Bill stood in the doorway, tray in hand. "Cappuccino, loaded with whipped cream, just the way you like it. Only I had them add a little brandy to help warm you."

"More brandy?" Cara opened one eye and squinted at the man who towered above her. "You'll have to carry me out of the tub."

He sat on the edge, proffering a tall glass mug. "I could do that," he said.

Cara thought his voice sounded funny, but then decided that was because hotel bathrooms always echoed.

She lifted one arm from the suds and reached for the drink. She sighed and smacked her lips. "Delicious," she murmured as her eyelids drifted closed again.

Bill stared at her, unable to lift himself from the tub rim. She'd exposed one breast when she'd reached for the glass. One round, perfect globe that glistened wetly as its pink nub grew full and pert in the contrastingly cool air above the steaming water.

Cara opened one eye and glanced down to her chest. And then she opened the other and raised them both to stare at Bill, who was gazing helplessly at her exposed breast. With great effort, he tore his eyes from her chest to meet her stare.

She felt her mouth go dry as her lower parts seemed to become heavy and achy. Without thinking, she slid upward against the tub, bringing both breasts to the surface, and set her drink on the floor.

Without thought, Bill reached his hand out to caress the silken skin that beckoned him. The nipple moved against his palm, and he closed his hand around the firm orb.

Cara moaned and started to slip back into the water, taking Bill's hand down with her.

They stared into one another's eyes as Bill's hand left her breast and smoothed down her belly to the apex of her thighs. Cara's legs, almost nerveless with pleasure, drifted open. Bill leaned forward, his shirtsleeve immersed in water, his hand following the bounty Cara offered. His own moan joined with hers, echoing off the tiled walls.

"I hoped this wouldn't happen, Cara," he whispered hoarsely.

"I hoped it would," Cara said. She sat upright then, suds sliding off her upper body, revealing more of herself to Bill. She was fully restored to sober wakefulness as she began to undo the buttons of his shirt.

His body was as beautiful as she remembered from watching him in the pool. Only then, he'd been wearing swim briefs. Without them, he was masculinity personified. Well muscled, little body hair, visibly erect, he stood unselfconsciously at the side of the tub. She stood up in the tub, her body covered with soap suds, and caressed the length of him, back and front, with lathered hands. With a cry of intense hunger, Bill pulled her from the tub, holding her up above his body for a moment before letting her slide down the front of him. Her body was slick with water and richly oiled bubbles that slid off her to expose patches of golden skin that made Bill's mouth water with anticipation. He bent to press his lips to those places, kissing and nibbling without thought to anything but the taste of her, while she held his head and moved her body to allow him better access. She was sunshine and scented soap. A taste he was quickly becoming addicted to.

It wasn't until she began to slip from his embrace, moaning impatiently, that he realized they were going to need more room. He lifted her up into his arms and moved swiftly into the other room, toward the king-size bed.

"We're going to get the bed wet," Cara protested, but Bill shushed her, his mouth clamping down on hers, and she immediately forgot about the state of the bed.

No doubt about it, Cara had the body of a goddess. He knelt above her and paid homage to her satin skin, her silken hair, her long limbs. She lifted and arched beneath his stroking hands and suckling lips, using both to bring her to trembling heights of ecstasy. She would have expected to fall limply back, sated to the point of exhaustion. But, instead, her body continued to hum with desire, and her mouth and hands longed to repay his generosity.

Bill had no intention of letting this become a feast to merely satisfy lust. Gently, he drew her back up his body so that they were face-to-face. He held her face in his hands and kissed her trembling mouth, tasting the honey of her, the nectar of himself, and then, with a triumphant cry of joy, he turned her onto her back and plunged himself into the depths of her. Their cries mingled as they climaxed together.

IN THE MIDDLE of the night, Bill unfolded himself from the lovely prison of Cara's arms and legs and slipped out of the bed, despite her sleep-murmured cry of protest. He bent over the bed to caress her shoulder gently, and she drifted deeper into sleep, with a soft smile on her face. He got into his clothes and very quietly crept across the room to the door. He eased it open, holding the doorknob in position as he closed it soundlessly, and then very carefully turned the key in the lock so that it made only the tiniest click in the quiet night.

The hotel garage was all dim light and shadows at any time of the day or night, but seemed more so at this unholy hour, with no other people astir and no cars coming or going.

He went to the trunk of his car and removed the briefcase, noting with satisfaction the feel of its heft against his thigh as he carried it at his side to the elevator doors.

The pneumatic hiss of the opening doors loomed loud in the silence, and he looked over his shoulder uneasily. Nobody out there. No way anyone could know where he was at this particular moment. Maybe they'd catch up with him by morning, but by then he'd be on the move again—if the early-morning news revealed what he expected, that is.

He retraced his steps, entering the building through the garage door, which opened onto the third floor, overlooking the glassed-in swimming pool. For some reason the deserted pool below looked almost spooky at this hour. He shivered and then made a wry face at his unaccustomed show of nerves. Still, he felt just then that he'd never want to swim in that pool.

But that was a moot point. They weren't going to be staying here more than another couple of hours, anyway.

He crossed the carpeted hall to the elevators and touched the up button. Its *ping* rang out noisily. He entered the elevator and pushed the button for the fifth floor.

Satisfied that he was alone in the halls of the fifth floor, he went to the door marked Stairs and eased it open. Quietly he crept up the tiled staircase to the sixth floor. He held his ear to the door and listened before opening it onto the foyer across from the sixth-floor elevators.

By the time he reentered their room, his chest hurt from holding his breath for so long. He let it out on a long, relieved sigh, forgetful of the sleeping figure in the bed.

Cara sighed in response to the sound she heard through her sleep, and she turned on her side and hugged the pillow against her breasts.

Bill put the briefcase on the top shelf of the closet and slid out of his clothes before creeping back to ease into the bed beside Cara.

She sighed again and turned back, discarding the pillow and pushing her naked body against Bill's.

She came awake with a jolt, crying out in response to the unexpected coldness of his flesh.

"Why so cold?" she mumbled, rubbing his chest, as if to warm him with her hand.

"Covers must have slipped off," Bill whispered, hoping she'd go right back to sleep.

Her hand moved down his body. "What's with the shorts, Bill?" she murmured.

"Got up to go to the bathroom." He waited, thinking she'd fall back asleep now. Her hand rested on his abdomen, warm through the cloth of his briefs. Inert. Heavy.

He began to breathe easier, just as her hand suddenly began to move. And then he found himself praying she wouldn't go back to sleep.

THE MAID FOUND THEM entwined in each other's arms, sleep-drugged from the previous day's dichotomous mix of horrors and wonders.

Cara came awake first, at the muffled cry of surprise from the maid.

"I knocked," the woman said, clearly embarrassed and frightened that her faux pas might cost her job.

"S'okay," Cara mumbled, pushing her tawny hair off her face. "We were up late."

"I'll come back," the maid said nervously, backing out of the room."

"Hour," Cara promised sleepily.

She laid her head back down, but by then Bill was awake.

"I've got to get up, hear the news," he said, sounding almost brisk for having just that moment come awake. "Do you need the bathroom, love?"

"Mmm-hmm... You first," Cara mumbled, snuggling farther into the warmth of the bed.

Bill got up and went into the bathroom. The sound of the shower snatched Cara back from sleep, Bill's words echoing in her thoughts.

The news. She jumped from the bed and turned on the TV as she wound the bedspread around her body in a makeshift sarong.

Bill was just coming out of the bathroom, his torso wrapped in a towel, as the announcer described the explosion of the day before. "And at this time, the authorities confirm that the explosion was caused by a gas leak in the boiler that served the building with hot water.

Fortunately, no one was killed in the incident," the anchor said, turning to his cohostess with a smile.

Bill turned off the set and went to the window.

"It's okay, isn't it, Bill?" Cara asked as she came up behind him.

Bill looked out over the city and rubbed his chin thoughtfully. "Hand me a cigarette, will you, Cara?" he asked, without turning around.

"Uh-oh," Cara said, "that's a bad sign, isn't it?"

Bill turned to face her. "What?" His sober look changed to one of amusement, and he laughed. "Oh, right. No, don't worry, that was just an ex-smoker on automatic pilot. Forget the cigarette, love."

Cara studied his face, his eyes, looking for the truth. "It is all right, isn't it? You do believe it was an accident?"

"Believe it? Sure. It's not likely the authorities would cover it up, if it were anything else."

"So we can go back to work?"

Bill brushed the riot of gold curls off her face and kissed her nose. "I'll call us in, let them know we're all right, in case they've heard the news and are worried about us. And we'll need the day off to look for another apartment and to shop for new clothes."

"Okay, I'll shower while you call." Cara kissed his cheek, tugging affectionately on his beard, and went to the bathroom.

Bill stood a moment longer at the window. He thought he could almost make out the lingering smoke above the apartment building across town. So it was an accident, after all. That added up to coincidence. He didn't like that. And yet it made perfect sense. A faulty boiler in an old building that the owner didn't spend a lot of money on for upkeep. The super was so lazy, he'd have overlooked any warning that the boiler was leaking gas.

Bill's chest tightened as he thought of the tenants in the building. It was some kind of miracle that those people had escaped with their lives intact. He had to believe that even Alvaretti was incapable of ordering a hit of such magnitude. It would take a real monster to wipe out all those innocent folks just to get at Bill Spencer.

Alvaretti was mean, evil, but even he wouldn't do anything that sloppy and unnecessary. He had access to enough good marksmen that he could get Spencer without taking out a whole building.

Bill turned to the phone. For the moment, he was still safe, and his life with Cara could go on as before. He heard the shower go on in the bathroom, and then the sound of Cara humming a show tune. Well, maybe not quite as before.

Better. Definitely better.

Chapter Eight

It was a miracle that nobody had been killed. Cara silently thanked God for the umpteenth time as she listened to the newscast while folding their new clothes into the suitcases they'd purchased. The people on the roof had suffered various injuries, but none of them were life-threatening, and none of the other tenants had been in their apartments when the boiler went off.

She and Bill had found a small furnished house for rent just a few blocks farther from the boardwalk. It was a tiny house on a minuscule lot, so close to its neighbors that in some ways it would be like living in the apartment building. Many of the streets in Santa Cruz were like that, with houses seeming to topple over on one another, as though there just weren't enough land for all the houses that needed to be built there. It reminded Cara of resort towns on the East Coast, where lake and ocean property was at a premium, and people were desperate to have even a tiny part of the land abutting the water.

Cara worried that it was too expensive, but Bill had argued that it was worth it, that it was safer. Safer how, she hadn't questioned. After their lovemaking last night, she was feeling putty-soft in the hands of the man who had proven to be an extremely exciting and tender lover.

But even that aside, so far he'd established that he was able to take care of both of them, though she thought he went a little overboard on the side of caution. His reaction to the explosion was a good example. He'd certainly overreacted there. Of course, it wouldn't have seemed so if he'd turned out to be right.

She put the last of the suitcases by the door, ready for when Bill returned to get her.

She decided to keep busy by checking the room to make sure they hadn't forgotten anything. She looked under both beds and found one of her earrings. Feeling justified in her thoroughness, she searched the bathroom and then the nightstands.

Nothing else. She was about to sit down when she thought of the closet.

That was where she found the briefcase.

She pulled it down off the shelf and stared at it. Was it Bill's? It looked like the one Bill had carried when they first met.

She hadn't seen it since...

Funny, she couldn't recall the last time she'd seen it.

She carried it to the bed nearest the window and set it down.

"Not since we moved into the apartment," she remembered suddenly.

But was it the same one? Was it Bill's? If it wasn't, it ought to be turned in to the desk, so that the rightful owner could reclaim it when he discovered he'd left it behind. But, of course, first she should wait to ask Bill if it was his.

She left it where it was and went to sit in a chair.

She watched a couple of minutes of a game show, but found her attention being distracted by the briefcase.

Black leather. Was Bill's black? She thought so, but maybe she was mistaken. Maybe it was brown.

She got up and changed the channel. Another news show. This time the reporter was talking about a rash of arson cases in Palo Alto. Arson. That was when someone deliberately set fire to a building. For profit, for kicks, to cover other crimes. Like murder.

She shivered and turned the dial again. A talk show. Not her usual fare, but harmless entertainment.

At first, she couldn't get a handle on the show's topic, but after a few minutes it became clear that one of the women on the show had been married to a serial killer and hadn't had a clue until the police came to arrest him.

Cara stood in front of the screen, her hand inches from the off button, but she didn't move, didn't take her eyes off the picture.

"Come on," the show's host argued, "are you saying that you could live with this guy, sleep with him, for ten years, and never even guess he was that kind of monster?"

The woman was almost in tears. "He wasn't a monster around us," she insisted. "Bruce is one of the most sensitive, caring guys I've ever met, and any of our kids or friends would say the same."

The host turned to another woman on the dais. "Let's ask our expert, police psychiatrist Dr. Daniel Fein. What do you say, Dr. Fein, could Bruce have been the angel Meg says he was at home and then go out and kill other women?"

"Serial killers are twisted on the inside, not on the outside, where it shows, Michael," the police psychiatrist said. "If they didn't appear to be normal—even sensitive and caring, in some cases—it'd make our job of tracking them down a lot easier. They don't have outward signs that point them out as murderers, unfortunately. You can't point at any given felon and say that's a bank robber, that's a car thief, that's a child molester."

She wasn't aware of pushing the button, of the screen going dark and blank, of the silence filling the room. The words of the psychiatrist reverberated in her head.

They don't have outward signs that point them out as murderers.

Her heart seemed to have leaped into her throat, and her ears filled with the sound of her own blood rushing through her veins. She literally felt her way to the chair, unable to focus on the room around her.

At what point had she decided to overlook all the warning signs and join forces with a stranger, one who was obviously running for his life? When had she forgotten that Bill was, in all probability, a criminal of some kind? Bile rose in her throat and her stomach lurched as she thought of last night's intimacy.

Desperately her mind searched for alternatives. It wasn't only a sexual thing. She'd also been attracted by his thoughtfulness, his many kindnesses, his obvious intelligence.

If they didn't appear to be normal—even sensitive and caring, in some cases—it'd make our job of tracking them down a lot easier.

She was reminded of Douglas Harvard. He'd certainly pulled the wool over her mother's eyes. Her mother was an intelligent woman, and yet she'd been swept away by the charismatic Harvard, while at the same time he'd shown an entirely different face to Cara.

A sob caught in Cara's throat. Was she destined to meet only men who were wicked or weak? And which was Bill Hamlin? Wicked? Weak?

Helplessly she gazed around the room. How could she have let herself get caught up in a relationship with a dangerous stranger?

Her gaze came to rest on the briefcase. It was Bill's. She was sure of it now. And for some reason she was sure it held the secrets Bill was hiding.

There was no hesitation on her part when she went to the briefcase. She was going to look inside.

It was locked. No surprise there. And no deterrent to her determination. She went to her purse and retrieved the little Swiss army knife she'd won at the arcade when she played the electric crane machine.

It took some effort, and more than one of the tools to pop the lock. She was surprised by her success, jumping in alarm at the sound of the lock snapping open.

The contents were even more surprising. First of all, there were three thick stacks of currency, two of them made up of hundred-dollar bills. Mouth agape, she stared at the stack in her hand, wondering how someone came to carry this much cash. And then her eyes fell on the gun, its handle sticking out from under a letter-size manila envelope. She lifted the envelope to make sure that it was actually a gun she was looking at. She'd never seen a handgun in her life. It looked lethal. She shuddered and backed away from the briefcase, then laughed harshly. Did she think the gun could go off on its own?

She could visualize the gun in Bill's large, capable hand, pointed at some unseen victim. After all, everyone knew you didn't have a gun around unless you were prepared to use it. And this was a concealed weapon. Wasn't it a felony to carry a concealed weapon?

She became aware that she was still holding the manila envelope. She felt no qualms about looking inside.

She'd already seen enough to prove Bill was a felon. Felons had no rights. Certainly not the right of privacy.

There were three different sets of identification inside, each banded together with rubber binders, each containing a driver's license, a social security card, a passport and job résumés. Each in a different name.

She carried the papers to the chair and fell onto the seat.

Thomas Martin Jacobsen. William Allen Spencer. Gerald Victor Gaither.

Was any of them real? Was "Bill Hamlin" Bill's real name...and these others...

She looked at the driver's licenses. All had the same picture on them. It was like the old shell game. She shuffled the packets. Which one was the real Bill Hamlin?

Her mind drifted over the preceding weeks, starting with her meeting with Bill—or whatever his name was—on the bus.

To be fair, he'd warned her not to ask questions, not to expect any kind of friendship with him. Actually, his keeping to himself so completely should have been the first sign that he was dangerous. And then there was that fiasco at the motel in Mount View. So what if he'd had second thoughts and come back to untie her—his trussing her up like stuffed poultry and treating her like a foreign spy should have told her he was paranoid beyond redemption. It was the sure sign of a madman.

"I'm the one who should be locked up," she growled, jumping to her feet, oblivious of the papers falling to the floor. She stepped over them and began pacing the room, stopping to peer out the window every few laps.

"I walked right into his trap." She hit herself on the thigh. "I even suggested we join forces and live together as a couple."

She stopped at the window, craning her head to look down at the cars against the building in the lot. No sign of Bill yet. She still had time to decide what to do next.

She started back across the room as she considered her options. She could call the police, have them there waiting for Bill when he returned. Her heart lurched strangely at the thought. She pivoted, retracing her steps. She could grab her own bags and get the hell out of there before he got back.

"Yeah!" She spun around and went to the door, reaching for one of the suitcases. "No." She slumped against the door and put her hands in her face. That was the coward's way out. She was tired of being a victim, being a coward.

She'd run from Doug Harvard, from facing her mother with the truth. She'd left Doug access to her mother and her mother's money with nobody there to stop him.

She went back to the window. She would confront Bill, warn him that if he didn't turn himself in, she'd do it for him.

"Ha!" A bitter laugh became a strangled sob in her throat. Oh, yeah, and of course the big bad man would just throw up his hands and promise to turn himself over to the law and mend his ways, if only the little girl would believe in him. "Right."

She was so preoccupied with her thoughts, she didn't hear the key in the lock, didn't see the knob turn.

She screamed when Bill suddenly appeared in the doorway.

It didn't take Bill more than a split second to read the scene before him.

His briefcase open on the bed, money and gun spilling out onto the chenille bedspread, his papers strewn across the floor, the look of terror on Cara's face, her scream...

He strode to the bed and grabbed the gun. "Shut up!" he snapped. "Sit down!"

The gun, together with the harsh tone of his voice, was better than a slap in the face at averting impending hysteria.

Like a puppet whose strings had been cut, Cara collapsed onto the chair behind her, and her second scream froze in her throat, becoming instead a gurgle of fright.

Or so he thought. He made the mistake of turning his back on her as he swept currency back into piles and searched for the rubber binders.

She was on him instantly, her fists pummeling his back and head, her voice spitting words of derision, some he hadn't even known she knew.

"You...you..."

He dropped both money and gun, and spun around to grab her wrists.

Her body was flush against his, her head was bent back in submission, and for a fleeting instant he was reminded of their lovemaking the night before.

The memory disappeared as she hissed, "You bastard, you're going to pay for this."

"For what?" He pulled her closer, his face only inches from hers. "What am I going to pay for Cara?"

"You're a...a monster!"

Bill's short spurt of laughter only underlined his anger. "Yeah, and what is it that makes me a monster in your view?"

"You're a killer!"

He had to admit he was taken aback at that. He held both of her wrists with one hand, bent his knees and felt around behind him for the gun. He found it and waved it over his head. "Because of this? You found a gun in my things, and that makes me a killer?"

He didn't know if he was more outraged at her snooping or at her slanderous attack on his character.

"People don't have guns if they don't mean to use them," Cara snapped. "And why else would you be so desperate to hide your true identity?" She nodded her head at his beard, her face twisted with scorn. "It's obvious."

"Okay." He let go of her so suddenly she almost fell. He pointed the gun at her, sweat forming on his upper lip, as it always did when he held a gun on anyone, even an unloaded gun such as this.

"So you've got a make on me now. So how come you don't have the sense to keep your mouth shut? Aren't you afraid I'll kill you?" He was surprised that he was able to hold the gun so steadily, given the degree of his anger.

He'd been nothing but good to this woman; he couldn't believe she'd turned on him so completely, so suddenly. And which had come first? Opening the case and becoming suspicious, or vice versa? What had driven her to turn on him in the first place? He'd have sworn Cara would never go through his things. And he honestly believed that deep down inside she didn't think of him as one of the bad guys.

A woman didn't give herself with the abandon Cara had last night if she didn't trust the man she was with. Or did she? He didn't know that much about women, if truth be told. He could count on one hand the number of women with whom he'd been intimate in his life, and none with whom he'd been intimate as he'd been with Cara.

"You don't have to kill me!" Cara shouted. "Not when I'm of more use to you alive."

Pain shot through him, a physical thing that tore the breath from his throat and punched him in the stomach.

He lowered the gun and slowly pulled himself erect. He stared at her, jaw slack, eyes wide with disbelief. "Use to me? How?"

"This whole business," she spit out. "You. Me. Pretending to be married."

He would have laughed if he hadn't been so angry at the unfairness of her accusation.

"Aren't we forgetting who came up with this brilliant scheme, Cara?"

A look of uncertainty crossed her face, quickly replaced by one of relief as she came up with a retort. "You could very well have manipulated me into making the suggestion."

He did laugh at that, a scornful chuckle that barely cleared his throat before anger replaced it with a growl. "And just how did I do that? With hypnosis? Drugs in your food?"

"I don't know!"

She was backing away now, inching toward the door. Bill didn't know if he had the strength to jump up and stop her, even if he wanted to do so. Right now he wasn't sure he wouldn't rather have her disappear from his life forever. He couldn't remember anyone ever hurting him more. Automatically his hand went to his side, where a narrow scar was a constant reminder of a knife wound from his early days in the field. No, the physical pain of that couldn't touch the emotional hurt Cara was inflicting now.

Cara stopped moving and pointed at the open briefcase. "I never thought to ask you where you were getting all the money you used to get us situated here. Honest citizens don't carry that kind of cash around, for Pete's sake. And honest citizens don't have to hide behind multiple identities!''

Her righteousness rang out in a clear voice, vibrant with barely concealed hysteria.

It occurred to Bill that she, too, was on the edge, that she, too, was suffering. Of course. Whatever had driven her to open his briefcase, nothing would have prepared her for the shock of what she'd found there.

He realized then that he was hopelessly trapped in a way he'd avoided all of his adult life. He was in love, and on the verge of making a commitment, one from which he'd never be allowed to escape.

Too late. He might love her forever, but he could never act on it, because if Alvaretti found out, he'd use Cara as another means of getting even with him. No, what he had to do was get her situated and then disappear from her life once and for all.

If she left now, with little money, no home, maybe no job, because she thought she had to hide from him . . .

He stood up, his carriage stiffening with resolve. ''So what are you going to do?''

''I . . . Get away from you.''

Her chin was thrust forward. Quivering, but nevertheless thrust forward with feigned courage. The absurdity of the situation struck him unexpectedly. Her anger, her courage, her threats, were all based on a fantasy. He was no killer. Granted, he still didn't feel he could tell her the truth, but it was a far cry from what she thought of him.

For the first time since he'd entered the room, his face softened, and he almost smiled. ''I don't think so.''

"Oh, really? And how do you plan to stop me? Tie me up? Shoot me?"

"I think when you come to your senses you'll realize that I could never hurt you, first of all. And secondly, nothing's really changed. You know little more about me now than you did originally. Why should you walk out now? You've found a gun, but that in itself doesn't make me a killer, does it? You've found a large amount of money, but does that prove I'm a thief?"

Cara's face reflected her confusion. She shrugged, but didn't answer him.

He lowered his voice seductively. "Cara, my love. Can't you continue to take me on trust? Nothing's changed. You've known I was on the run from the beginning. All you've learned from the briefcase is the means by which I'm able to keep going and to protect myself, if that becomes necessary."

Cara let her breath out on a long, heavy sigh and turned to the window. Dusk was beginning to dull the colors of the day, and she felt inertia beginning to set in.

"What do you want from me?" she asked over her shoulder.

"I want us to go on as before. We still need each other—that hasn't changed."

"You make a good argument." Her tone was flat. She turned back to face him. "But I can't help it, Bill, I feel as if I would be naive to just ignore the contents of that briefcase as if I'd never seen it." Her voice turned pleading. "Can't you tell me something more, set my mind at ease a little?"

"You want a guarantee." Bill locked the briefcase and set it down on the floor beside the bed. "I can't give you that, Cara. You're going to have to take me on faith."

Cara shook her head and rubbed her eyes with the heels of her hands. Fatigue bent her shoulders, and she collapsed onto a chair, a scowl of frustration creasing her brows.

"Why should I?"

Silence hung heavy between them. Then Bill whispered, "Because I love you."

It was hard to tell which of them was more surprised by Bill's confession. Cara saw the run of emotions reflected in his face and knew that her own face mirrored them.

It should have been so easy to say, "I love you, too, Bill." But there were too many unanswered questions hanging between them. And, even knowing he loved her, she wasn't sure she could take him on faith. Which made her wonder about her own feelings. If you loved someone, didn't you automatically take him on faith? She couldn't answer that, either. Now that she'd calmed down, she knew that she'd overreacted both to the TV show and to what she'd found in the briefcase. The bottom line was, she'd have staked her own life on the belief that no matter what else Bill might have done, he wasn't capable of murder.

That still left myriad crimes that he might have committed, and that knowledge didn't sit comfortably on her shoulders.

She got to her feet. "Let's go. I'd like to get settled into the new house before it gets dark."

"Does that mean . . ."

"It doesn't mean anything, except that for the moment I'm willing to go on as before. How I'll feel tomorrow, or a week from now, I can't promise."

Her last barb, thrown over her shoulder as she bent to pick up her suitcase, hurt Bill the most. "And when I say go on as before, I mean before last night."

AN UNEASY TRUCE formed between them as they settled into the little house. Since they now worked different shifts at the park and didn't take meals together, Cara was usually alone when she was at home, and it was easy to pretend the house was all hers. When she thought about Bill living there, she quickly made herself think of him as a kind of boarder. In her mind, the house belonged to her.

And she made it hers—buying colorful prints for the walls, covering the shabby furniture with throws, putting lamps in dark corners and shiny glass pieces on various tables around the rooms.

They'd long since come to know each other's food preferences, and without a word exchanged, she always bought apples and peaches—his favorites—for the fruit bowl, and he always left a carton of sweet and sour pork in the fridge for her when he'd eaten Chinese.

She bought bagels for him. He left mocha-flavored instant coffee on the counter for her. She replaced his peanut butter when it was gone, and he added blackberry to the jams he knew she liked.

If she held the jar of jam against her chest for a few moments before returning it to the lazy Susan, who was there to see, to question?

There were two bathrooms in the house, so they didn't have to share that intimacy, and for that Cara was grateful. She didn't think she could stand to see the razor that carefully shaped his beard or the towel that wiped dampness from his masculine chest. She didn't have to step onto a throw rug, damp with his footprints after his shower. And she didn't have to wipe his toothpaste out of the sink before she brushed her teeth.

There was only one problem. Every single time she looked at her bathtub, she was reminded of another tub, in a hotel room across town. It took an effort, but she forced herself to push the memory away as quickly as it came.

They exchanged no words—spoken or written. If there were messages inherent in their food gifts, they were never acknowledged or admitted.

Bill came in later than usual one night to find Cara asleep on the couch, her head crooked to one side and falling off the couch cushion, the book she'd been reading open across her chest. He knelt beside her and very carefully lifted her head onto the pillow.

She opened her eyes and stared at him. "What are you doing?" she asked in a raspy whisper. The book slid off her body onto the floor. They both ignored it.

"Your head was bent awkwardly. I was afraid you'd get a stiff neck," he whispered back.

"Nice," she murmured, her eyes drifting shut. "Thanks."

"Yeah." His hand was still at the back of her neck. He could feel the soft vulnerability there, sense that she was totally relaxed and only barely aware of the situation. Her lips were enticingly sleep-swollen, her cheeks flushed pink. He could smell the warm, soapy fragrance that lingered from her shower.

If she was awake, she'd attack him ferociously for what he planned to do, but she was asleep—or almost—and he couldn't resist, even if she whacked him a good one for it afterward.

He leaned forward and lifted the light summer blanket down to her waist and bent to place his lips at the hollow of her throat. She was wearing a white cotton gown with spaghetti straps, and her breasts curved enticingly above an inch of ruffle. His lips inched along satin skin to those curves, and his tongue paid homage to the honey-sweet taste of her.

Above his head, her lips breathed out a sigh of pleasure, and she arched her back in such a way as to give him greater access to the bounty he sought. Bill lifted his own head and saw that her eyes were still closed and she appeared to be sleeping still.

But when he glanced down, he saw that her nipples were erect, their thick buds poking through the light fabric of her gown. Without thought, he bent to suck one of those buds into his mouth, and his body seemed to shimmer with pleasure as his tongue rolled around it.

It was Cara's moan that told him she either was awake and willing or thought she was having a very lifelike erotic dream. Her hands sought the silkiness of his hair, and she lifted her body to his marauding mouth.

He pulled the gown to her waist and pushed her breasts together so that he might have the pleasure of both nipples at once.

Cara cried out and clutched his head to her breasts. She had awakened, realized she was not dreaming. Every cell in her body seemed to hum with ecstasy; there was no way to recall her anger, to deny their hunger for one another.

Her hand began to slide downward, when suddenly a horrendous noise broke the late-night silence, bringing them both to their feet. Cara snatched up the blanket to cover herself and followed on Bill's heels as he fled to the rear of the house from where the noise had come.

The sky was awash with moonlight. The neighboring houses, surrounding theirs in such close proximity, cast grotesque shadows over the white-lit grass. Across the backyard, a cat howled in angry frustration, and another feline leaped over the wooden privacy fence and up into the branches of a lemon tree.

Nothing else stirred. No sound of runaway footsteps, or the revving of a car engine. Nothing was disturbed on their screened-in porch.

Heaving a sigh of relief, Bill turned back, prepared to reassure Cara that all was well and that they could resume their lovemaking.

But Cara was gone. And when he went into the house, he saw that her gown had been removed from the floor beside the couch and her bedroom door was shut.

She'd changed her mind, come to her senses.

Bill went to bed alone after a punishing cold shower, and morning brought more of the same silence, as though the brief interlude of passion had never occurred.

Chapter Nine

Bill bit the last of the corn dog off the stick and threw the remains in a trash barrel. It was turning out to be a slow day, and he had been eating junk food out of sheer boredom.

Something had kept people from turning out in the usual large numbers. As an easterner, he found it hard to credit the overcast weather for the diminished activity on the pier, and even if it should rain, it didn't threaten to be more than what New Yorkers called 'a slight drizzle.' But it was soon clear that the locals didn't see it his way. Which left mostly the heartier tourists who hailed from the Midwest and other, more eastern parts of the country.

During one of the many slow periods that morning, Bill ambled over to the edge of the bumper-car concession and glanced up and across the boardwalk. Cara was at the ice-cream cart looking almost as bored as he felt. She was sitting on her stool, her feet resting on the bottom rung, her chin in her hands as she gazed out past the boardwalk to the beach area and the ocean beyond.

Was she imagining herself aboard one of those fancy yachts or on a steamship headed for foreign ports? Was she, at that very moment, wishing she'd never met Bill

Hamlin and could be enjoying a different kind of life here in Santa Cruz?

She turned, as if she sensed his gaze on her, and he quickly averted his eyes and bent to pick up a candy wrapper from the sidewalk.

After a few minutes, he dared another look and saw she was filling cones for two little boys, who were jumping up and down with excitement. Her grin when she placed a cone in each child's hand struck an unexpected blow to his solar plexus. It seemed forever since he'd seen that sunshine-bright smile, and a lifetime since it had been directed at him.

He turned away and walked under the roof that covered the bumper cars. Four children and three adults had positioned themselves in the cars that were lined up along the perimeter of the corral. Bill went to the edge and began pushing cars away from the rail. Usually he did that task so quickly and with such absorption that he barely noticed the occupants of the cars. But this time, as he was pushing the green one away from the rail, something drew his attention to the boy seated in the car.

He found himself staring down into the most arresting green eyes he'd ever seen. It wasn't just the amazing color, or the incredible lushness of the thick black eyelashes, that caused Bill's breath to catch in his throat. The boy's eyes contained such a look of profound sadness that Bill felt drawn down into a mire of despair, just looking into them.

"You okay, kid?" Bill cleared his throat, surprised at the huskiness in his voice.

Several expressions crossed the boy's face. First there was surprise, and then, as he glanced over at his parents, terror. And then his face settled back into a frozen nonexpression that was more unsettling than even that fleeting look of terror.

Bill shrugged and turned away. He vaulted the rail and walked toward the controls.

"My imagination," he muttered to himself. "I'm beginning to think like Cara."

But all during the ride's cycle, Bill couldn't tear his gaze from the green car and the boy with the matching eyes.

The kid looks familiar, a voice inside his head whispered. *Nah, I've just been staring at him too long.*

Bill tried to distract himself by glancing over at the people around the outside of the arena. The two people he'd figured to be the kid's parents were huddled together against the wall, staring at their son as if they were afraid he was going to disappear in a puff of smoke, right before their eyes.

Just regular overprotective parents who'd heard too many horror stories about what happened to people on vacation.

Suddenly, Bill realized that they didn't have the usual look of vacationers. There faces were set in grim lines and, come to think of it, there wasn't the usual look of parental pride in their eyes as they watched their son.

They aren't having any fun, Bill thought.

"Not even the kid," he mumbled aloud, turning to look back at the boy. The child sat in the car, hands on the wheel, letting the other cars bump into him, doing nothing about fighting back, not even trying to escape the other fun-seeking drivers. All the other drivers, adults and kids alike, were having fun.

All but the lone youngster with the haunting eyes.

Damn! Where have I seen those eyes—that face—before?

The cars were slowing now, as the ride was about to end. For some reason, Bill gave the timer an extra twist, causing the mechanism to rev back up to full speed, keeping the ride going, keeping the boy there a little longer.

His ploy for extra time didn't help. When the ride came to an end, he still hadn't figured out why the child looked so familiar.

Strangely, the kid's parents rushed to the car and dragged the boy out, the way some parents had to do when a kid refused to believe the ride was over. Only, in this case, the boy wasn't showing any interest in staying on—he hadn't shown any in the first place.

They left the concession with the boy in the middle, Ma and Pa each firmly clasping a spindly arm.

That should have been the end of it.

But as they walked away, the boy looked back over his shoulder and gave Bill the most tormented, pleading look Bill had ever seen on another person's face—a look unlike any he would ever expect to see on the face of a child.

He couldn't help himself. He followed the trio out to the boardwalk and watched as they walked up the pier. The boy's head never turned to take in the sights. He never pulled his parents in the direction of a ride, a food booth, a games concession. The three of them trudged along as though they were playing the parts of tourists on holiday.

And playing them badly.

They stopped when they got to the ice-cream cart. The man turned to look down at the boy, and Bill saw him ask the boy a question. The boy's shoulders lifted in a half-hearted shrug.

The man said something to Cara and then nodded in a questioning way to his wife. Cara scooped ice cream into two cones. After she handed them the cones, and while the man was getting out his money, Cara knelt down and looked into the boy's face. She said something, and the boy nodded slightly. She said something else, but this time there seemed to be no response. She stood up, and Bill saw that there was a peculiar expression on her face.

Suddenly, he was impatient to know if she'd reacted as he had to the child. All thoughts of their cold-war status were forgotten as he went back and locked the control box, hung the Back in Five Minutes sign on the chain across the entrance and dashed up the pier to the ice-cream cart.

It wasn't until he was facing her closed-off, cold expression that he realized how foolish he'd look if he questioned her about the boy. "Not very busy," he said, knowing how inane it sounded.

Cara shrugged, mumbled something indiscernible and turned away. She kept her face averted as she busied herself with scraping down the ice-cream well that contained chocolate.

"Not many customers today, eh?" he persisted.

Silence.

"Noticed you had the same customers I did just now."

A curl of ice cream slid from the plastic wall to the center of the tub.

"Strange-looking group, wouldn't you say?"

Cara looked up then, a frown of irritation on her face. "Why are you here making small talk?" she demanded. "And since when are you so interested in any of the tourists?"

It was the opening he needed.

"Did you think they were tourists?" he asked eagerly.

The look of irritation turned suspicious. "What's with all the questions, Hamlin? What do those people have to do with you?"

"Nothing." He wasn't sure. And he thought he'd sound foolish trying to explain, so he didn't bother. "Just curious."

"Yeah, well, that's curious in itself."

She slammed the lid on the chocolate container and shoved the scoop into a container of water.

She was occupied with drying her hands when Bill asked, "What did you think of the kid?"

She gave him her full attention then, staring into his face. "Is this some kind of joke? Or maybe it's your feeble attempt to restore a friendship between us." She snatched up the scoop again and threw open another lid. "I can assure you, Hamlin, that isn't going to happen!"

His own temper was on the rise. This woman could be totally unreasonable. And here he was, making a fool of himself, and all over a tempest in a teapot. What the hell did he care about the kid or the parents or any of the other fools who came through here on a daily basis?

"Forget it," he snapped, turning away. "Sorry I bothered you with an innocent little question about one little boy."

"Nothing you do is ever innocent," Cara said disgustedly.

Bill decided to ignore that; there was no way he was going to win with her. He headed back toward his own concession.

Forget her, and forget the kid!

He realized then that she was shouting something after him. He turned and caught the tail end.

"... wasn't a boy, it was a girl."

How like Cara, needing to get in the last word, even when she'd made it clear she wasn't talking to him.

He stopped in his tracks, his hands plunged deep in his back pockets. People pushed around him, and the sound of the calliope starting up drowned out anything else Cara might have called after him. He turned back, but she was already busy with another group of customers.

A girl? Had he heard her right? Surely not. The kid had what could only be described as a boy's haircut, complete with a side part. He wore a sweatshirt under overalls and had on high-top sneakers—boys' clothing.

Bill resumed his job at the bumper-car controls, but his mind felt storm-tossed as he played and replayed his memory of the child he had assumed was a boy and Cara had tagged as a girl. That, in itself, would have kept him in a quandary. But the memory of those eyes—tormented, pleading—made the whole thing far more important than a mere puzzle.

Bill's relief man showed up at two. "Front office said to tell you to take off for the rest of the day, Hamlin. The crowds are down, and it looks like rain, so we're shutting down earlier than usual."

Normally Bill would have gone back to the little house, puttered around, taken a nap, read the paper, maybe gone shopping if there was something he needed or wanted, or he would have mowed their postage-stamp-size yard.

Today he hung around the boardwalk, not sure why.

He stopped at the gyro stand and had a sandwich, keeping his back to Cara, who was only a few feet away. He thought about other times when they'd shared a break, shared a meal, shared walks, drives, sex...

He threw the remains of his sandwich in a trash basket, strode in the direction of the park, and was soon settled on a park bench. The air had become moister, the sky more overcast—a definite prelude to rain.

The subject was on everyone's mind. "It's only going to drizzle," a man's voice proclaimed from the next bench over. Bill turned in that direction.

They were a young couple with a child of about four. Boy? Girl? Bill really couldn't tell what, with the short curls and the unisex romper suit.

It seemed this was his day for noticing kids. This one had blond hair and bright blue eyes. Pretty kid, but not arresting, like the boy at the bumper cars.

Boy? Girl?

He slouched down, his legs out before him, his head resting on the back of the bench, his hands shoved in his pockets. Damp air chilled his face, and he could feel drops of moisture clinging to his beard. It felt good. He dozed, the amusement-park noises from the distance all coming together to form a single white sound in his mind.

He dreamed.

He was back at his agency's headquarters, where he and his co-workers were swimming in a room filled with computer printout pictures. As he silently dog-paddled through the paper, the faces of the other agents distorting and receding around him, one picture seemed almost to jump into his hands. As he held it, it turned from a printout to a color glossy. Bill stared at the picture with a sense of recognition, but just as he was about to shout his findings, the paper around him became water and he was being sucked down to the bottomless depths.

A splash of water in his face jolted him awake. Bill jumped up from the bench and saw that most of the benches were empty. The dampness had turned to drizzle and gathered in puddles on the leaves of the tree limb that hung out over his bench. He took out a handkerchief and wiped his face.

Screams rang out from the direction of the roller coaster over on the boardwalk. An eerie sound when coupled with the music of the calliope. He shivered and started back toward the casino.

He saw the trio then—the man, the woman, and the child of questionable gender. They were crossing the park, heading toward the parking lot. The child's eyes met Bill's, and once more he was struck by their silent message of anguish.

In that instant, the child's face seemed to shimmer and change, and suddenly Bill was seeing a picture of another child. A child with long, dark curls and huge, round green eyes bordered by thick dark lashes and dark eyebrows that formed two peaks to emphasize those amazing eyes.

Kelly Parton. Seven years old. Missing from her home in southern California following a 6.6 earthquake. The Parton home had fallen in the wake of the tremors. One minute she'd been with her parents in the crowd standing around the rubble of houses on their block, and the next she'd just disappeared. Two weeks later, she still hadn't been found, and the cops had been calling it a snatch. APBs had gone out all over the country. The local FBI office had been called in, and pictures and pertinent info had been faxed to the other agencies' branches.

The information came flooding back to him.

Bill stared after the trio. They could cut her hair and dress her in boy's clothes, but they couldn't change those eyes, and Bill felt sure that those were Kelly Parton's eyes.

Either that or Kelly Parton had an identical twin. But there'd been no mention of that in her background.

His feet began to move of their own accord as his mind struggled through the influx of memories. He'd seen the picture while he was waiting for his chief to call him into his office. He'd expected to be assigned to the case. Instead, he'd been told he was going undercover on the Franco Alvaretti case. The biggest career move an agent could hope for—the chance to bring down one of the nation's five leading capos.

The couple were pulling the child along as they drew closer to the parking lot. Bill increased his speed so that he was loping across the grass now.

Over two years since the Parton girl had been snatched. She'd be about nine now. He kept his gaze on the threesome as he reduced the distance between them and himself. Would he know a nine-year-old from one younger or older? He wouldn't. But he could make an educated guess that the child ahead of him was about nine.

Too bad the kid hadn't had any fun on the bumper cars. Kelly Parton had been smiling in her picture. A smile was a real identifier.

But maybe not. In the picture, Kelly's front teeth had been missing—two on the top and two on the bottom. At nine, she'd have all her second teeth, and her smile would be quite different.

They were about fifty feet ahead of him. His lope became a sprint. Forty-five feet.

There wasn't any question about what he intended. He had no plan as such, but he kept going.

And then what?

He pushed the thought away as if it were a pesky fly.

Thirty feet. He could hear them breathing. Or was it his own breath, its volume increased by exertion?

The man was small, spindly, older than Bill by maybe ten years. Bill squinted, rubbing perspiration or drizzle from his eyes. Bowed legs. Good. The man wouldn't be able to run as fast as him.

Twenty feet. Now Bill knew how he was going to do it.

The gap closed. His feet pounded on asphalt, and the couple and the child halted and turned to see where the noise was coming from. It was the reaction he'd counted on. Surprise.

He never broke his pace. One minute he was in front of the trio, and the next he was past them, the child's body held firmly against his own as he ran.

Vaguely he heard their shouts above the sound of his breathing, the sound of his feet on pavement. He kept going. He heard car horns honk as he ran against red lights, but he kept running.

He began to chart a course, to make a plan. He turned off one street and down another and then turned onto another and another, altering his usual route home, making it impossible for anyone behind him to guess at his next move.

But was there anyone behind him? He wouldn't look back, wouldn't lose one second of the advantage he had. He kept running.

First he'd get home, get his car. Was there more than one set of feet hitting the pavement? He tightened his grip on the little girl and picked up speed, but he didn't waste time looking back. His chest was beginning to burn, and his mouth felt dry as sand. He worked his tongue, trying to raise enough saliva to wet his throat, but he never slowed his pace.

The child whimpered against Bill's chest, but he didn't look down. His only response was to move his hand to the back of the child's head. He didn't break his stride.

He turned a corner running at full speed, the house a few feet ahead. He could see the broken screen door at the back.

He was going to make it! Exhilaration gave him a second wind, that extra burst of speed he needed to get himself and the girl safely into the house.

And then what?

No. No time to worry about that now. First he had to get Kelly Parton off the streets and then he'd figure out what to do next.

He turned into the small backyard and moved quickly toward the back door.

CARA ENTERED THE HOUSE and jiggled the key out of the lock before kicking the door shut behind her. She was just about to reach for the light switch on the wall when she heard the sound from the back of the house. Her hand halted in midair.

Bill? But it couldn't be. Bill wasn't due home from work for another two or three hours.

She heard the sound again. "Bill?"

Her heart was pounding as she heard footsteps coming from the back of the house.

Just as she flipped on the switch, flooding the kitchen with light, Bill appeared in the doorway, gasping hoarsely, a strange-looking bundle clutched to his chest.

It took Cara a moment to adjust her eyes to the light, to understand what she was seeing.

The grocery bag in her arms slipped to the floor unheeded, and a scream tore from her throat when Cara recognized the little girl in Bill's arms.

Chaos ensued. The child in Bill's arms came to life at the sound of Cara's screams, and she, too, began to shriek. Bill spun in a circle, attempting to put the child down, wanting to go to Cara, uncertain of how to proceed.

He started toward Cara. "Cara, love, please listen. It's not what you think..."

But Cara backed away, still screaming, her hands pressed to her mouth, her eyes wide with fright.

He tried to disencumber himself of the child, but she only screeched louder and clung to him with surprising strength.

When he saw that there was no other way to gain control, to restore order, Bill stuck two fingers in his mouth and whistled shrilly.

The two females froze, their screams echoing in the suddenly silent kitchen.

Bill set the child on her feet and gave her a look that defied her to move from the spot. When he saw obedience in her face, he turned to Cara, who was slumped against the island, attempting to regain her breath.

"This child is Kelly Parton," he told Cara.

Cara looked from him to the child and back again, a blank expression on her face.

"You don't remember the Parton case?"

She shook her head.

"Following an earthquake in L.A. two years ago, Kelly Parton was snatched right out from under her parents' noses."

As if she'd just recognized her name, Kelly whimpered, and the two adults turned to her in unison.

"You are Kelly Parton, right, honey?" Bill asked.

The little girl nodded and then began to sob. Both Bill and Cara moved toward her. Cara got there first and lifted Kelly up into her arms.

"It's okay, hon," Cara said softly, patting the child and rocking her as if she were an infant.

Bill put his hand out to touch the child, but Cara spun away, glaring at him over her shoulder. "Don't even think about it," she snapped.

"What? Hey, Cara, I'm the one who brought her here, remember?"

"Only too well."

She moved across the room with the child, putting the island between herself and Bill.

Her voice was more bitter than he'd ever heard it. "And now I know why you were so desperate to keep from being found, and where you got all that money."

Bill shook his head. "The money? What's the money got to do with anything?"

She started across the room toward him and then caught herself and stopped where she was. "The ransom money, Bill Hamlin, or whatever your name is!" she cried. She banged the counter with her fist before placing her hand on the child's head again.

"I thought I was out of line thinking maybe you'd killed someone." Her voice rose. "Silly me! You'd never kill anyone. No, you're better than that, aren't you?" She almost screamed the words as tears began to stream down her cheeks. "You're a kidnapper, a child molester!"

She fell back against the counter, hugging the child tight to her bosom. "When I think that I slept with you, made l-love with you . . ."

Bill was around the island in a flash. "You can't believe that, Cara, you can't think I'm responsible for kidnapping that child!"

He put his hand on her shaking shoulder, and she wrenched away. "Don't touch me, Hamlin! And don't touch her." Her voice was cold, steady, though the tears still dripped, unheeded, over her smooth skin. Her brown eyes brimmed with more of them, waiting to spill.

He wanted to use his fingertips to brush the tears away, to assure her that this was all a mistake, a bad dream.

But it was clear she believed it, and it was also clear she wasn't going to hear a word he said to her until she got all her hysteria out of her system.

He went to the table, pretending a calm he didn't feel, and took a seat.

"Think about it, Cara," he said in a tired monotone. "How could I have kidnapped the Parton girl and held her captive all this time? I've been with you for the past month, for heaven's sake."

"I don't know. I haven't worked it out. But you must have been in cahoots with that couple."

Her voice grew stronger as her imagination kicked in. "I thought that business with the little girl was strange this afternoon. When you came over and asked about them."

Bill stared at her, willing her to a logical summation. And waited.

"I thought, why is Bill so interested in those people? It isn't like him to show any interest in anyone, really."

Bill was taken aback by that. He started to open his mouth in protest, but thought better of it. She wasn't through yet.

"I realize now, you wanted me to think the girl was a boy. You made a big fuss over that. I know now—you were passing the child in front of me as a sort of test, to see if people could be fooled into thinking she was really a boy."

"Wha-at?" The chair crashed to the floor as Bill leaped to his feet. "That's patently absurd."

"If it's so absurd, how did she get here? What are you doing with her?"

Bill bent to pick up his chair and gestured toward the other one. "Come and sit down, and I'll tell you."

The child had fallen asleep, her head nestled on Cara's shoulder, and she was becoming increasingly heavy for Cara to hold. Cara eyed the second chair at the table with longing.

Bill raised his hands, palms out. "I won't touch either of you, I swear."

Fatigue won over doubt. She sat down, and Bill began to talk.

Cara wanted more than anything in the world to believe him. She didn't know if it was that desire, or the mesmerizing quality of his voice as his tale unraveled, that diminished her doubts.

For Bill, seeing the change of expression in her eyes was enough. He had only lied a little, telling her that he'd learned about the Parton kidnapping from television news spots. Apart from that, he had told the truth, and she recognized the sound of it.

"What were you planning to do next?" Cara asked, stroking the boyishly cut hair on the sleeping child's head.

"Call her parents and make a deal. No media, no cops, no heroics. They get their little girl back, and I disappear underground again."

"Why not turn her over to the police?"

"Cara, nothing's changed for me. I can't bring myself to the attention of the authorities, especially with this, which can only lead to TV coverage, among other things."

"Do you think the Partons will believe you?"

Bill shrugged. "What choice do they have? I'm their best bet in over two years."

"You're going to have them come to Santa Cruz?"

"Yeah. I thought I'd arrange to meet them at the airport. While they're preoccupied with their reunion with Kelly, I can make a quick getaway."

Cara thought about it. "You're going to have to call them from a public phone. Why don't I fix Kelly something to eat, and we can be ready to leave when you get back?"

"No!"

"No? No what?"

"I can't take you with me. This has to go down very rapidly. The Partons get off the plane, I meet them, lead them out to the car, hand over Kelly. I'm gone."

"So, I'll wait in the car."

"Cara, if something goes wrong, you'll be be suspected of being my accomplice. I need you to stay out of it."

They argued for a few more minutes until Bill said, "I may need your help getting me out of trouble if anything goes wrong, so I need you on the outside of this."

"Help you how?"

"I don't know exactly. But what I thought was, you wait here. If I'm not back by the time I'm supposed to leave for work in the morning, you go to the boardwalk personnel office and wait for a call from me."

Cara hesitated only a second before handing the sleeping child over to Bill so that she could fix a meal. They discussed the pros and cons of Bill's plan while Cara scrambled eggs and made toast for Kelly, who ate ravenously when they awakened her. Though both of them spoke to her, she never answered, except to shake her head now and then.

They made quiet small talk while the child ate. After drinking her milk, she set her glass down, looked up at Bill and asked, "Are you my mommy and daddy?"

The question sent shock waves rumbling through Bill's chest. He knelt beside her chair and touched her head tenderly. "Kelly, don't you remember your mommy and daddy?"

The child's face creased with confusion. "Sometimes. But mostly I can't think of their faces."

"Listen, Kelly. My name is Bill, and this is Cara." Bill gestured toward Cara, who had paled in response to the child's question. "We're... I'm going to take you back to your parents."

Kelly cringed. It was Cara who realized why. She jumped up and came to kneel beside Bill, taking the little girl's hand in hers.

"Bill is going to take to you to your real parents, honey. To Mr. and Mrs. Parton."

"Will I remember them?" Kelly asked in a small voice.

"Oh, honey, I promise, when you see them, you'll remember, and you'll remember how much they love you and you'll see how happy they are to get you back." Bill's words came out on a stifled sob.

After that, if Cara had any doubts about Bill's involvement in the matter, they were immediately obliterated. She found a sweater for the child and walked with them to Bill's car and then leaned in to kiss the child's cheek before they took off.

Almost as an afterthought, she went around the car and leaned in through the window to kiss Bill soundly on the mouth. "Good luck," she whispered. "I'll be waiting for you."

Chapter Ten

Bill leaned forward to peer past the windshield wipers at the road sign.

Kelly was asleep again, curled up in the corner, her head on the armrest, her hands clenched in fists under her chin. His heart thumped an extra couple of beats as he stared over at her in the dim dashboard light.

Poor baby. God only knew what horrors she'd suffered at the hands of those weirdos, not to mention the initial horror of being torn away from her parents. Like Dorothy in the tornado, she must have thought the earthquake had sent her to another kind of Oz.

He drove along Route 1 until he came to a gas station with a phone attached to the exterior wall.

There were twelve Parton listings in the Santa Monica area, according to the information operator. Did he have a first name? He didn't.

He hung up and stood for a minute, deep in thought.

The logical next move, if he was an ordinary citizen, would be to take her to the nearest police station.

Did he dare risk it? Would they let him turn her over and then just walk out? Not likely. They'd spend hours grilling him. And they might not believe his story even then. Hell, they'd probably run his fingerprints. No, he couldn't risk that.

He went inside for more change for the phone and bought a carton of milk and a box of crackers. As an afterthought, he went back for a package of Twinkies, something he recalled from his own youth as the perfect treat for a kid. When she woke up, Kelly would probably be able to eat again, and he had no idea how long this whole thing was going to take.

His second choice was just as frightening as calling the cops, but he decided he had no other option. With shaking fingers, he dialed a phone number that was indelibly engraved on his memory. He heard the official greeting and was about to make his request when an operator came on the line and asked for money to be deposited for the call. The clanging of coins registering made him think of the sound of a cell door clanging shut, and he shuddered and dropped one of his coins.

"I need to speak to Chief Brinkers," he finally said.

There was a pause, and then the receptionist said, "Chief Brinkers is no longer with this agency. May I direct your call elsewhere?"

So Paul Brinkers had finally retired. Now what? "Can you tell me who replaced him?" he asked.

"May I ask who's calling, please?"

"I...just..." He cleared his throat, shook his head, and tried again. "I need to speak with the bureau chief," he insisted. He hoped he sounded peremptory enough to daunt her.

"Chief Hart is not in," the woman said.

Hart. So Tim Hart had made it to chief. Not surprising. Bill remembered how officious the agent had been. Definitely better suited to the desk than the field, though unfortunately not the leader of men that Brinkers had been. Did he want to butt heads with Hart?

"Listen," he said, returning his attention to his call, "I know it's not usually done, but can you give me Hart's...er...Chief Hart's home number?"

Her brief chortle mocked his naiveté. "I'm sorry, sir, we don't just give out private numbers. If you'd like to give me your name and—"

He hung up. He'd known it was useless to ask. There was only one other person he could call, but before he did so, he glanced over at the car. The little girl was stirring.

Bill went around to the driver's side and slid behind the wheel. "I got you some food, honey," he said, opening the bag. "Eat this stuff, and if you want something else, let me know."

"Thank you," the little girl said in a small voice.

"Kelly, is there any chance you remember your real parents' address or phone number?"

Kelly scrunched her face up in concentration but then shook her head. "Do you know their first names?"

Kelly shook her head again. "I can't remember," she whispered, her voice gravelly with sleep.

"Okay, kid, don't worry about it." He patted her head and then opened the milk and passed it to her.

It dawned on him that there was a question she could answer, though it wouldn't help him locate her parents.

"Kelly, the people who had you at the boardwalk today—what are their names?"

Kelly lifted her mouth from the milk carton and stared at Bill, her eyes luminous with fear. "Are you going to take me back there?"

"Oh, no, honey. Cross my heart. But I need to know their names."

"Her name, the mom's, is Grace...Gracie. The dad's is Hoyt."

"Hoyt. What about his other name?"

Kelly shrugged and pushed at the flaps of the carton with nail-bitten fingers. "Dunno."

Bill sighed and told himself to be patient. What would Cara say to the child? "Kelly, didn't anyone ever call those people...Gracie and Hoyt...Mr. or Mrs.?"

Kelly nodded.

"Good. Mr. or Mrs. what?"

"Mrs. Hoyt."

"Oh? So everyone called Hoyt by his last name. Did you ever hear his first name?"

Kelly shook her head.

"What did Gracie call him?"

"Hoyt."

It was the best she could manage. Bill opened the box of crackers and handed it to the child.

"Listen, honey, I have to make a phone call. You eat, and I'll be right out there at the phone."

He dialed the number, a different kind of dread stirring in his stomach.

He could see Kelly through the windshield, scarfing crackers and drinking deeply from the milk carton.

"Devon Glade."

His ex-partner's voice was as deep, as compelling, as Bill remembered. He also remembered the man's look of stoic Scots determination. Glade owed him a favor from years ago. It was time to collect.

"It's Spence, Dev," Bill said softly, surprised at how easily his own name fell from his lips after using the alias for so long.

"Spence? Bill Spencer. My God, it is you."

"Yeah. It's me." His insides seemed to be twisting into knots. "I need some information, Dev."

"Wait a minute, Spence. Where are you? Are you all right? Do you want us to bring you in?"

"Dev, Dev, whoa, fella. I'm fine, and no, I don't want... Listen, Dev, I just need an address."

"An address." The pause was laden with unspoken questions. Like "Why should we give you information when you're no longer one of us?"

He glanced over at the car and saw that Kelly had slowed down. She was getting full. She'd probably be nodding off again soon.

Bill held his breath and then let it out in a long sigh. The best way to handle this was to jump right in.

"Dev, I need the address of the parents of Kelly Parton, the Kelly Parton who was snatched right after that earthquake in L.A. a couple years back."

"Parton? Why in hell—"

He heard a crash over the line and realized Dev had jumped to his feet and knocked his chair over. He hadn't expected this to be easy, but he also hadn't expected fireworks.

"Look, why don't you come in—or, better yet, why don't we meet somewhere and..."

"The address. Do I get it or not?"

"Aren't you going to at least tell me what this is all about?"

Bill looked over his shoulder before answering. He'd been right. The girl had fallen asleep, her head resting against the window. He had to get her off his hands, get himself back on track.

He turned back to the phone. "I'll tell you this much, Dev. I've found the Parton girl."

"Wh-at! Jeez, how did you manage that? We've been looking for her since— Oh, hell, you're pulling my leg, right?"

"No, Dev. I've found her. Got her. Only now I don't know what to do with her. She doesn't remember much about her family, and—"

"Where are you, Spence?" Glade said, interrupting. "We'll take it from there."

Bill shook his head. "No way, Dev. I've got my own butt to cover. All I want is that address... No, better yet, get me a phone number."

Another long pause. He knew Glade was weighing the pros and cons. Deciding whether this had to be played by the book.

"I'll have to make a phone call, Spence. Do you want me to call you back?"

Bill chuckled. "No thanks, old buddy." He glanced at his watch. "How long will it take?"

"Still playing it close to the chest, eh, pal? Okay. Give me fifteen minutes."

They hung up, and Bill began pacing in front of the phone, his mind in turmoil as he worked out the logistics of returning the child without blowing his own cover.

And what if Glade let him down? He hadn't seen his old friend in a few years, and people changed in less time than that.

It was with great trepidation that he dialed the number again twenty minutes later.

Glade was waiting for his call.

"They're right off Route 1. In Ventura." He gave Bill the number.

"Thanks, Dev. We're even now."

"Yeah, well, I've wondered when you were going to call in your marker. Listen, Spence, be careful. Doing a good deed could turn on you, blow up in your face, you know?''

"Yeah. Thanks, Dev. I'll be careful."

He dialed the long-distance number and fed coins into the slot. As he waited for the call to go through, he thought of Cara. How excited she'd been when he told her what had happened, who the child actually was, that his intention was to return her to her real parents. It had broken the ice between them, at least made her see him as less of a monster. Maybe now she'd quit looking for trouble where there was none.

BILL SHUFFLED HIS FEET and watched as the small plane made its landing on the wet runway. Funny, most of California came to a grinding halt when it rained, but there had been no doubt in Paul Parton's voice when he said, "Don't worry, we'll be there in three hours."

Kelly was still asleep, so Bill left her locked in the car outside the little airport and went to wait for the plane by himself.

It was a small chartered plane. The Partons were the only people who deplaned, and Bill was surprised to see that they were middle-aged. He'd expected the parents of a nine-year-old to be younger.

When they drew closer, he saw that they only appeared older because of the worry lines permanently etched in their faces. Would those lines ever go away, even when they had their child back?

He put out his hand.

"Bill Hamlin, sir. Kelly's right outside the terminal in my car."

It seemed to Bill that the other man hesitated briefly before accepting his hand in greeting. He glanced over at Mrs. Parton, a small, dark woman who seemed to hang back behind her husband's arm. Peculiar. But maybe not, considering what they'd been through for two years or better. They'd probably had their hopes raised over and over, only to have them dashed repeatedly.

He led the way out of the building. The car was right there at the curb. Kelly Parton was still asleep, her face pressed to the window. Bill thought he'd give them a moment alone for their reunion. He handed Parton the car keys.

The couple spotted the child, cried out in shock and delight, and almost knocked Bill over in their rush to get to their child.

He took a step backward. He altered his original plan on the spot. He was right to leave them alone. He started to turn away. He'd go inside, have a cup of coffee, give them maybe twenty minutes, half an hour. Parton would know enough to come inside and get him when—

They seemed to come at him from everywhere. Armed cops stepped out from behind him, guns drawn, faces set in grim warning.

"Freeze, Hamlin!" one of them called out.

He froze, more from surprise than from fear of the law. The surprise lasted only a moment. The fear set in when one of the cops stepped forward and began to read him his rights, while another stepped behind him and cuffed his wrists together.

THEY GRILLED HIM for hours. He'd started out determined not to give them a clue as to his real identity—that much he could preserve. But after a few hours he knew they could very well arrest him, and if they did, they'd fingerprint him. And once they did that, it would only be a couple of hours before they learned his true identity.

The world would learn his whereabouts. And then so would Franco Alvaretti.

His only prayer was that they'd believe his story about the couple who'd had the child and had actually gone out to look for the couple and found them. Meanwhile, he was their prime suspect in the two-year-old kidnapping.

"I tell you, I just saw the girl for the first time today." He glanced down at his watch. "Yesterday." Confused, disoriented by fatigue and nerves, he shook his head. "I've told you guys all I know, the way it really happened."

Another uniform came into the interrogation room and whispered something to the detective who was questioning Bill. He heard fragments of sentences. "No record... Description... Chief says... your call..."

"Am I under arrest?" He needed to close his eyes, to gather his strength so that he could think clearly, figure a way out of this. Even if he got that rest in a cell on a jail cot.

The detective seemed to come to a sudden conclusion. "You're all we've got, Hamlin, and you had the child. That's all the evidence we need to hold you for now, fella."

"Do I get a phone call?"

"Sure. After we run through your story one more time."

CARA STOOD by a heavily screened window, hugging her arms around her waist. She felt cold, even though sunshine flooded the room and a warm breeze blew in through the open window.

"Cara, thank goodness you came." He rushed to the window, and they embraced, but Bill could tell Cara's heart wasn't in it. He stepped back and lifted her chin with one finger.

"What's wrong, love?"

Her teeth were chattering. "I can't believe they're holding you in here."

Bill grunted. "Yeah, well, I knew all along it was a risk." He extended his arm behind her and put his hand on the window frame, bracing his weight. He bowed his head so that she could hear his whisper. "Did you bring the briefcase?"

Cara nodded. "Do you think it will come to that? Court and bail and everything?"

"I hope not. Most of it will depend on how much they believe you, how convincing you are. Or if they actually go looking for the Hoyts and find them."

"The Hoyts?"

"Yeah. Kelly told me that was the name of the couple who had her. I told the cops that, but I'm not sure they believed me. Anyway, I haven't seen any signs that they're out beating the bushes for those weirdos."

Cara shivered again. "What if they don't believe me, Bill?" Her eyes and voice were bleak.

"They've got to believe you, love. It's my only chance of getting out of this without having my name splashed all over the papers and TV and before the FBI shows up to take over the investigation."

"Yes, but Bill, I only know what you told me."

"Cara, you know the child wasn't anywhere near me before yesterday. Also, you were there when I asked Kelly who she was, so you know I didn't know the kid before that."

Cara frowned and rubbed her forehead. "Why can't they just ask Kelly? Surely she would be able to tell them she never saw you before yesterday."

"Cara, she's got to be one very traumatized child. They aren't going to let anyone—not even the cops—grill her before she gets some counseling. It could take weeks before any doctor would consider her well enough to be questioned."

Before Cara could respond, the door opened and Inspector James, the detective who'd booked him, came into the room.

"We're ready for you now, Miss Davis."

They'd agreed the night before that Cara should drop the married act, given that the police would be less apt to believe testimony given by a man's wife, should it come to that.

Now that it had, Bill began to doubt that Cara's word would be enough.

Another cop was there to escort Bill back to the lockup. They parted company outside the visitor's room, hands and eyes clinging with quiet desperation—Cara fighting back tears, Bill biting back a stream of epithets at the unfairness, the stupidity, of the whole thing.

And then a small miracle happened as Bill was being led back through the detective's room to the lockup beyond.

The Partons were signing papers at a desk in the corner. Kelly Parton was sitting on her mother's lap, her head laid back against the woman's bosom, her thumb in her mouth. But when she spotted Bill being led toward the door, she left her mother and went running to Bill.

She threw her arms around him and craned her neck to look up and give him a huge smile. "Bill, Bill! I remembered them! I did! And they remembered me! Thank you, Bill, thank you!"

There were tears in Bill's eyes when he bent to touch Kelly's head. "You're welcome, honey. And I'm glad you remembered."

That little scene with Kelly was all that was needed to support Bill's story. Cara's corroboration was the icing on the cake.

Detective James released him.

"We just located the Hoyts a half hour ago, and we've taken them into custody. The feds are going to be here this afternoon to question them and do what they have to in order to tie up the loose ends of the case," he told Bill. He signed a paper and then lifted his head to meet Bill's eyes. "And as soon as the story breaks, this town is going to be overrun with media."

He glanced over at the Parton family. "The computer didn't turn up anything on you, Hamlin, and we haven't had time to run you through the feds' records, but I have a hunch you're hiding something, even if you had nothing to do with the Parton snatch."

Bill held his breath. Was the guy going to go looking for some reason to detain him?

James threw his pen down and stood up abruptly. "They parked your car down on the street in front of the station." He pulled Bill's keys from his desk drawer and tossed them to him.

"You're out of here, Hamlin. If I'm right about you, you don't have much time to cover your tracks."

THEY LEFT the police station together, holding hands and congratulating one another in whispers, unaware that the whole scene between Bill and Kelly had been photographed by a free-lance photographer, and unaware that he snapped a picture of the two of them holding hands on the steps of the police station.

"What now, Bill?"

"It's not over yet, love," Bill warned. "When this story breaks, I may be headline news."

"Does that mean we have to leave Santa Cruz?"

Bill led her toward the car. "I'm not sure. Listen, what did you tell personnel in terms of our working today?"

"Nothing. I didn't know, so I left it that you'd call if you were going to be late."

Bill glanced at his watch. "Good. We have over an hour before I'd have to report in. Let's go have breakfast, and we'll brainstorm."

They found a café a few blocks from the station that contained only a few patrons. They took a back booth and ordered, and Cara waited impatiently while Bill made a trip to the men's room to wash up.

When he returned, he looked more relaxed. He slid into the booth across from Cara and reached for her hand. "I think it's going to be okay."

"Really? How?" She massaged the knuckles of his hand with the pad of her thumb, enjoying the contrast of crisp hair against smooth skin.

"We're going to take a chance that James isn't going to blow my cover to the press. If he doesn't, we're right where we were before Kelly Parton came along. Since the media wasn't around when I was brought in, I think it's safe to trust that we may be able to stay."

"Then we can go back to work, and home tonight?"

The waitress brought their plates, and Bill let go of Cara's hand and raised his fork. "You got it, dude. Let's eat. I don't dare be late for work again, or I won't have a job to go to."

"I guess I'll go to the park with you and just hang out down at the beach until it's time to go to work myself," Cara said, pushing her eggs around on her plate.

Bill looked up from his own plate, surprise etched on his face.

"Why? You could take the car and go home and grab a couple more hours of sleep."

Cara stopped pretending to eat and put her fork down. She met his eyes with a look of naked emotion. "I don't want to go too far away from you today."

Bill stared at her. "Why?" he whispered.

Cara slid her hand into his and clung to it fiercely. "Because I love you, Bill."

Bill felt his insides lurch with a mixture of excitement and panic. He slumped back against the booth wall, though his hand continued to cling to Cara's.

"I know I'm the one who started this, Cara, but have you ever really thought about the dangers inherent in this situation?"

Cara looked puzzled. "I had the feeling that we were sort of out of the woods. I know now you're not a murderer and you're not a kidnapper or a child molester. I guess that means that whatever's left, I can live with."

Bill laughed. "But you're still dancing with the idea that I'm some kind of criminal."

A puzzled look crossed Cara's face. "Bill, we're lovers, we're in love, and I've proven I'm on your side. Can't you trust me even now?"

"Cara, can't you get it through your head that it's not a case of trusting you? It's as much to protect you as to protect myself that I haven't told you anything."

Cara nodded. When she spoke again, her voice mimicked his. "I know—the less I know, the less danger I'm in if whoever or whatever catches up with you."

She knew that stubborn look that tightened his features. Bill wasn't going to budge. But then he surprised her.

"I guess I can tell you some of it. But not now. I have to get to work." He took money out of his pocket and threw it on the table. "Come on, love. We'll talk later, I promise."

ACROSS THE STREET, Gordon Lefebre watched and wondered. He'd been surprised when he followed Cara and observed her entering the police station that morning. Then he'd been even more surprised to see her come out with Bill Hamlin. He'd debated whether to go into the precinct and nose around or follow the couple.

What had decided for him was the way the couple were behaving with one another. This was the real thing. He had no way of knowing exactly when, but sometime between that building exploding and his locating them at their new address, Cara and Bill had become lovers.

Now he had to decide if this was something he wanted to report to his client. He knew what he *should* do. The trouble was that his feelings kept getting in the way.

Hell, he didn't really know anything about their business with the cops, so there wasn't anything new he could report to the client, anyway. He'd already given the guy their new address and checked the premises to assure himself they still had no phone.

Still, this had been a lucrative assignment. Who knew when the client would need him again or have occasion to recommend him to someone else. He got into his car and eased into traffic, keeping Cara and Hamlin in his sights from a safe distance.

He'd make sure they were going to work, and then he'd check in with his client. Maybe their business with the cops had something to do with why the client was having them tailed.

CARA KEPT GLANCING across the boardwalk, trying to catch a glimpse of Bill, but the crowd that passed between the bumper-car concession and her ice-cream cart had thickened. The sun had been shining that morning, but now the sky was overcast, and it looked as though they might have another bout of rain later in the day. It was almost as if people had rushed to be here for the few hours of good weather.

Every now and then Cara would spot Bill's dark head above the crowd, or a flash of his blue shirt. A couple of times they had a clear view of one another and waved, Bill's eyes sending warm, seductive messages.

Cara was surprised that her feverishness didn't melt the ice cream before she could mold it onto the cones she sold. She kept thinking, *We're in love, but that doesn't mean all our troubles are over. There's so much I need to learn about him, so much he doesn't know about me.*

And yet, when she'd glimpse him through the passing parade, her heart would do flip-flops in her chest and her breathing would become erratic. And then she'd remind herself, *He's going to tell me. Maybe not everything, but something. And then I'll tell him about Doug and Mom and, who knows, maybe we'll be able to help each other through our problems.*

On the other side of the fairway, Bill was in his own little world. In fact, a couple of times, in his dazed state, he'd forgotten to set the timer and the ride had run way over the designated allowance.

He couldn't help thinking, *I love her, but the best thing I could do for her is to leave her. Only, God help me, I have to be with her just a little while longer. I need just a little more time before I have to give her up.*

He used his afternoon break to go home and take a nap. When he started back to the park, he saw that the clouds had thickened and the sky had darkened.

He stopped at the ice-cream cart, and the way Cara looked at him made him shove his hands in the back pockets of his jeans to keep from touching her right there on the job.

"You're some hot-looking tootsie," he whispered.

"You silver-tongued rascal," she whispered back. "You keep talking like that and I might start groping you right here in front of everyone."

"Oh, man, I love when you talk grope," Bill said, with a groan that proved he was only half kidding.

"You want me to talk ice cream?" Cara asked teasingly. She flipped open one of the wells, scooped some strawberry onto a cone and moved it toward her mouth, her tongue flipping out to start the first lick.

Bill snatched a hand out of his pocket and pulled her hand down toward the cart before the cone reached her tongue, causing the ice cream to fall off the cone. "Stop that, you little tease! I've still got a couple of hours of work ahead of me."

Cara threw the cone into the trash and wiped her hands. "Okay, I'm on my best behavior now," she said calmly. She lifted her face and gave Bill one of her sunniest smiles.

Bill cleared his throat and swallowed hard. "It looks like we might get rain tonight. If we do, I'll get off early. Why don't you wait for me at Antonio's, and we'll have dinner together?"

Cara shook her head. "Why don't I go on home and fix us dinner?" Her grin was wicked. "That way, we'll already be home if we find we can't wait to finish dinner before we start on dessert."

Bill groaned. "You make it very difficult for a guy to concentrate on his job, lady."

Cara laughed and then glanced around before chancing a brief tug on Bill's beard. "Go be stoic, Hamlin. I'll see you at home."

Chapter Eleven

Gordon Lefebre was sitting in the the bar area of a restaurant when the news bulletin came on. "Turn it up, quick," he commanded. The bartender obeyed and went back to the blender where he was mixing cocktails for a party of bridge players.

"Our sources tell us that at first Mr. Hamlin had been mistakenly tagged as the kidnapper of Kelly Parton. However, not only did Mr. Hamlin find and return Kelly to her parents, but information he gave the police led to the arrest of the real kidnappers, Grace and Clarence Hoyt. We will continue to update you as more information comes to our attention."

Lefebre drained his glass with a sigh of satisfaction, both for the drink and for the turn of events.

The irony! Only this afternoon the client had discharged him from the case, telling him his services were no longer needed.

And only this morning he'd wondered about their business at the police station. And now the information had been handed to him, gratis.

He chuckled and raised his hand. "Barkeep, let's do this again," he called out.

His end-of-assignment dinner—the treat of a fine meal at a rather elegant restaurant, nowhere near the beach. He was growing weary of the grittiness of sand on every surface, the smell of fried foods clinging to his clothing, the sight and sounds of the tourists bringing themselves to mental orgasm over the inane rides and games.

Now he stared at the screen, musing over this new turn of events. Should he call the client one last time and tell him about this? He didn't know why, but he had a feeling it would piss the client off. He wouldn't mind one last jab at the guy, who, though faceless, had come across the wires as all ego.

"Emotional poop is not acceptable, Gordo," he whispered over the rim of his glass. The surface of the liquid shimmered under the force of his breath. He thought about the girl. Cara. How he'd love for her to join him in just such a place, sharing a decent decanter, a gourmet meal. He'd spoken with her only briefly, asking directions, back in Utah, at the motel. He had no idea if her intelligence warranted getting to know her, but he'd heard her voice, with its husky quality, and that alone had intrigued him.

"I do believe you're smitten, Gordo," he said under his breath.

The barman looked over, eyebrow quirked.

Lefebre waved off the barman. "I'm fine," he mouthed. He'd enjoy the remains of his drink and then allow the maître d' to show him to his table for a leisurely dinner. Plenty of time. Cara's shift didn't end until eight, so he still had a couple of hours. He could always catch up with her later. After all, he wasn't officially on the case any longer. He was marching to his own drummer now, and for his own motives.

SHE'D FELT as though someone were following her from the time she left the boardwalk, passing the Coconut Grove, where Neptune's Kingdom was situated. There hadn't been the usual blast of noise from the place, because the crowd at the park was less dense than usual. It was only eight o'clock, but it was already dark out because of the overcast sky. She'd heard footsteps, but when she turned to look, she'd seen nothing. Across the street, an elderly couple had been hurrying toward the corner, huddled in their jackets as if the mere misting were a downpour.

Cara tried to think about how much she'd always liked this kind of fine rain when she lived in New England. Her dad had taken her for walks in the rain when she was little, and when she got older, she'd enjoyed going out alone in it, letting it cleanse her face and spirit. Nothing depressing about rain, as far as Cara was concerned.

She looked over her shoulder again. She was almost away from the bright lights of the amusement park, almost to the street where she turned to get to the little house. It was what she missed about the apartment building. It had been only a couple of blocks from the park, with the walk well lit all the way.

The damp air had caused her hair to pull loose from its braid, and it kept falling across her eyes. She pushed it away and looked back again. There was nobody nearby. No tourists, no residents. The lights from the boardwalk seemed to blur behind the curtain of fine rain.

Nobody. And yet she was sure she heard footsteps behind her. There was an echo of them when she stopped, as if whoever was following her had stopped just a heartbeat after she did. She didn't want to waste time looking over her shoulder, but she couldn't help herself.

She had to know if there was someone back there, see the face of her stalker.

Was that a shadow moving at the side of that building?

Nothing. She hurried on.

It had to be her imagination. She knew it was her most uncontrollable personality flaw. She could take the least little nothing and build a scenario way out of proportion to the truth. In fact, she'd even had teachers suggest she'd make a good writer.

It was a dark and stormy night....

"Cut the crap, Cara," she muttered aloud. "You're only scaring yourself."

She quickened her pace. Three more blocks to home. She had always heard that in California everybody had a car, nobody walked. Yeah, right. Well, whoever said that hadn't been to Santa Cruz, where walking was practically a local sport.

"So where are all the walkers tonight? Afraid of a little rain?" she said aloud. "Afraid their little California tans will fade if they get wet?" She laughed, and then deliberately laughed louder. Maybe whoever was behind her would think she was crazy. That'd scare him off.

She spotted the market up ahead, its light spilling onto the street, pooling the wet street with puddles of neon red, green and purple. The light gave her a sense of security. She'd duck in there and shop a little, maybe schmooze with the owner, an elderly lady, if she was there tonight. Some nights her grandson worked the shop, and he wasn't nearly as friendly.

Once inside the shop, she could watch the window, see if anyone suspicious went by. Feeling safer, she hurried across the street and down the block.

The grandson was reading an adventure novel and barely glanced up to greet Cara. Disappointed, she nevertheless smiled and called out a comment about the weather. It was comforting just to be in the brightly lit store, and when she thought about it, she decided a grown man was better protection than a frail elderly lady.

"Bad for business," the man grumbled. His bald pate glistened under the fluorescent light overhead and made him look as if he were sweating, despite the cool temperature in the store. He returned to his paperback.

Cara took her time, browsing the canned fruit section at the front of the store, and then moved to the side wall, where she could see out into the night through the plate-glass window.

She'd almost given up, sure the whole thing had been her imagination, when the man came abreast of the window and peered in. Cara jumped back and quickly hid behind a pyramid of soup cans.

It was the man from Mount View. The man from San Francisco. And now she was sure it was the man she had spotted across the boardwalk the previous week.

Could it be coincidence? She didn't think so, but one thing she knew for certain—she wasn't going to throw herself across his path.

She took a chance and peeked out. He was gone.

She began to move out from behind the display.

I don't believe in coincidence. Bill's words came back, almost as if he was right there inside her head.

She stopped and looked around, feeling helpless. Was the guy out there, waiting for her, waiting to waylay her on the walk home? If he'd been following her all along, he knew where she lived. He could be there ahead of her, waiting to ambush her on the porch. Maybe he'd gotten inside and would grab her when she entered the house.

He had to be one of the people Bill was running from. He couldn't be following her. She was pretty sure she hadn't left a trace. Besides, if her mother had sent someone to find her, that person would have let her mother know the minute he discovered her whereabouts. By now, her mother would have arrived to beg her to come home. Or at the very least, Beth would have asked the detective to confront Cara and insist she call home.

So, the tall, well-dressed, good-looking guy was one of Bill's people.

Automatically stalling for time, she began to gather things from the shelves. The bell over the door rang, and she jumped and dropped a can of tuna.

She knelt to retrieve it and then got slowly to her feet, peering over the top of the shelving to her right. Two young women were at the counter buying cigarettes.

The bell rang again as they left the store. She glanced over to her right and noticed the door marked Emergency Exit.

She took a couple of deep breaths and forced herself to think calmly. She could go out that side door and double back to the boardwalk. Bill would be there, as well as the other park employees, not to mention lights and tourists.

She shoved the items she carried onto a shelf and made for the side door. She heard the grandson call out, but she didn't stop to reassure him.

She began running in the direction of the pier, sure she'd be safe once she arrived there. Bill. She had to warn him. They'd have to get away.

One block down, three to go. She ran on. Her shoulder bag thumped against her hip, and she held it in place with one arm, using the other for balance as she ran.

One block left. The lights weren't much brighter, and the rain seemed to be increasing.

She was on the sidewalk leading up to the boardwalk now. And as she dashed through the rain, headed for the walkway leading up to the bumper cars, she noticed that many of the rides and concessions were closed.

That accounted for the dimmed lights. The park was shutting down early because of the rain.

In a last burst of panic, she rounded the corner and saw that the bumper-car concession was dark, the chain across the entrance, the Closed sign in place.

She fell back against the wall of the dark corral and waited for her breathing to return to normal. Now what? The ride must have closed shortly after Mr. Gambrini relieved her.

Mr. Gambrini!

She ran out from under the ride roof and peered through the rain, up the boardwalk. Her shoulders slumped. None of the concessions in her area were open, and no other people were visible. She was about to turn back when she saw movement far ahead in the sky.

The Ferris wheel had moved, its lights shimmering in the rain-misted night. If that ride was still open, that meant there were still people up there who could help her. She ran down the walkway and around to the path leading to the end of the boardwalk farthest from Neptune's Kingdom.

Bill might be up there. His shift didn't end until the entire boardwalk closed. If any of the rides were still open, he might have been sent to work one of them.

She was almost there when she heard footsteps coming up behind her, running almost at the same pace as hers. Panic filled her throat and at that same moment she saw that the Ferris wheel was shut down, that only the lights remained on. And her foolishness came home to her then—the bumper-car concession would have been the last to close, not the first, because it was one of the few sheltered from the rain.

And now she was mounting the last boardwalk, and she was alone in the rain, in the night, and the footsteps were closing in on her.

BILL ENTERED the dark house and went through the rooms, turning on lights and calling out Cara's name.

No answer. In the kitchen, he found no sign of a meal being prepared. He glanced at his watch and frowned. Had he made a mistake? Were they supposed to meet at Antonio's? But no, he remembered distinctly her offer to prepare dinner and then...

He went back to her room and opened the door, thinking she might have lain down for a moment and fallen asleep. Or perhaps she was in her bathroom, showering.

The bed was empty, neatly made. The bathroom door was ajar, and the interior beyond dark.

"Cara, where the hell are you?" He tried to ignore the sudden arrhythmia in his chest. She'd probably stopped for groceries. Yeah. They'd eaten out so much that they hadn't stocked a whole lot of ingredients for any kind of a dinner. Especially a celebration dinner.

Which brought him back to the events of the past twenty-four hours. Despite the nap he'd had earlier in the day, he was suddenly overcome by fatigue. Maybe he'd lie down for a couple of minutes. He went to the front of the house to make sure the porch light was on for Cara and, as an afterthought, went out to look up and down the street.

The rain had increased. He couldn't see to the corner. He dashed back to the porch, wiping water from his face with his sleeve. Maybe the rain had held her up. She was probably at the store, waiting for a break in the weather, or maybe she'd had the sense to call a cab. Cabs would be scarce in this kind of weather, and she'd have to wait quite awhile, in all likelihood. For the first time, he felt truly frustrated because he hadn't bothered to put in a phone.

He got a towel from the linen closet and rubbed his hair and neck before going to his bed to stretch out. Just half an hour. She'd surely be home by then.

CARA LOOKED over the rail to the walkway below and saw a line of Dumpsters. She leaped over the wooden rail and scrunched down behind one of them, listening for the sound of footsteps. She had to strain to hear against the sound of rain and the ocean roaring behind her. She was surprised to find that what she heard was the screams of exhilaration and fear that always came from the Giant Dipper. Could that ride be open, even in the rain? It must be. If she could backtrack and get over there, she'd be safe.

She crept out from behind the Dumpster and began to inch her way down the walkway, listening carefully for any sign of her pursuer. The rain had increased yet again, and now the sound of it was like another presence in the night, tinny as it hit the roofs of concessions, thumping on the boardwalk, splashing when it hit puddles. Her wet hair, now completely free of the braid, clung to her cheeks, her neck and her back in heavy clumps. She shoved strands of it from her eyes and kept going.

The framework of the roller coaster loomed before her, a dark monster of a shadow against the night sky, the lights from below making it appear haunted. She squinted. She didn't see any cars on the loops, didn't hear sounds from the ride. Had she only imagined—?

A noise from behind her made her bolt up the next walkway. It sounded as if someone had crashed into one of the Dumpsters. She saw that she was near the river parking lot. Should she veer over there, look for people in their cars, maybe waiting out the rain?

Another noise, the sound of footsteps pounding the boards, running in her direction. She whimpered and looked around. A distant light beckoned. She moved quickly up the walkway.

A familiar smell assaulted her nostrils. Sweet, hot, enticing. A surge of relief flooded her being. The candy kitchen. It was just ahead, the lights blazing as if to welcome her in from the frightening night.

She ran toward it, almost crying out in relief. The candy people must be doing their last clean up, maybe even making candy for tomorrow.

It was a night-light.

The place was locked up tighter than a drum skin. She pounded on the door, called out.

She heard feet pounding the boards, and again she thought she heard screams.

Sea gulls? Protesting the rain? Did they come out at night? She looked around.

Other smells became noticeable. Frying-fat fumes, and the perfume of the cotton candy machine. She was near the hot-dog-on-a-stick concession, could almost smell them, too. The damp air seemed alive with aromas from the day's trade.

Her stomach lurched as a wave of nausea spread through her. She put her head against the wet, cold metal of the accordion window that folded down over the skeeball concession. Her heart felt as if it were beating in her throat, and her limbs ached from the exertion of running.

You can't stay here.

She lifted her head, looked both ways, and decided she had only one option. She had to head back toward the grove, toward Neptune's Kingdom and the Fun Center, where at least the usual bunch of teenagers would be gathered around pinball and video machines, shouting out greetings and comments in their peculiar slang. If she could just get back there . . .

BILL LOOKED AT HIS WATCH for the fourth time in less than ten minutes. This was ridiculous. He wasn't getting any rest, anyway. He might as well get up and do something constructive.

But when he got back out to the kitchen, he could think of nothing to do but to go looking for Cara.

He put his plastic rain jacket on, pulled the hood over his head and started out the door. He stopped on the porch. A note. He should leave a note for her, let her know that he was out looking for her, that if she came home while he was out, she was to stay put and not worry.

He wrote the note, propped it against the napkin holder on the kitchen table and went out to the car to trace the route he was sure Cara would have taken from the park.

CARA'S SCREAM rent the night as an arm became a manacle around her waist and pulled her up against the solid weight of a masculine body. The sound of her scream was aborted instantly and quickly absorbed into the night by the hand that clamped over her mouth.

She struggled against the superior strength and a voice in her ear grated out a warning. "Don't try it, lady. You won't get away."

Panic obliterated every sound, every feeling. Her mind was a kaleidoscope of fragmented terror as her assailant dragged her down the walkway.

Where was he taking her? Why didn't someone, anyone, show up? Who was this man? What was he going to do with her? Would he torture her to make her tell him where Bill was? But if he'd found her, surely he knew that she and Bill lived together.

Questions flew into her mind and then right back out as she struggled against her assailant.

Powerful arms pulled Cara over to the Dumpster. She fell against the metal wall and slid down to the ground. She scrambled to her hands and knees in an attempt to regain her feet and run. She caught her breath, prepared to scream for help.

He was on her again before she could run or scream. It was pitch-dark behind the Dumpster, which added to her fright until she realized she had her eyes squeezed shut in terror. She forced them open and was relieved to see that there was a dim glow of light reflecting off the wet walkway from the overhead lamps, though she couldn't see her attacker from behind her. She heard the snap of a blade being released from its hasp, and then a knife was thrust in front of her face.

"Go ahead and scream, lady. No one can hear you back here."

"Please," she whispered, "take my purse, I won't report it."

His laugh was maniacal. "Your purse? What have you got that I'd want, lady? You're worth more than a couple of bucks and a credit card."

"Wh-what do you m-mean!"

He pulled her around, and she got her first glimpse of him. He was small. That surprised her, somehow. He'd felt bigger as he hauled her across the boardwalk.

His face was mean—his eyes slitted, his mouth twisted downward, as if life were a permanent disappointment, his hair dark and plastered to his head as a result of the rain. She realized then that he meant to kill her. He'd done nothing to conceal his face, because she was never going to get a chance to identify him.

She moaned, a low, frightened sound. "D-don't. P-please."

His smile was more terrifying than his frown had been. "Go ahead and beg, lady. I like that. It makes an ordinary job more interesting."

He raised his hand. The knife blade glinted as it arced high above his head. She watched as it swooped downward, coming closer and closer to her throat.

A sudden rage filled her. He was going to kill her! This mean little man she didn't even know was going to take her life behind a Dumpster, leaving her body in a pool of blood surrounded by used paper cups and empty French fry bags.

She lifted her knee toward his crotch at the same time she opened her mouth and screamed at the top of her lungs.

The man's scream joined with hers, and he fell away and then sank to his knees in slow motion, the knife clattering to the ground.

Cara didn't register the sound of footsteps running up as she reached for the fallen knife. Her fingers had just begun to close around it when it was snatched away.

She looked up and saw the tall man who had followed her earlier standing over her, the knife now in his hand.

Beside her, the little man groaned, and she turned her head in surprise.

Two of them!

She opened her mouth to scream again, but this time she found she had no voice. A mere rasp escaped her burning throat.

"Wh-who are you?"

She was going to die. But not without knowing why and by whose hand.

The tall man knelt and put a hand on her head. She flinched, but when she tried to draw away, she found she was kept in place by the smaller man, who was curled in a fetal position beside her, still groaning in pain.

To her surprise, the kneeling man put the knife in his pocket and used both hands to grasp her arms and lift her to her feet.

"You're all right now," he said. "He didn't hurt you, did he?"

"I..." She put a hand over her eyes, confused and disoriented. She pulled her hand from her eyes slowly and stared at the tall man. "Who are you?" she repeated.

"Let's get out of this rain," the man said, urging her, with one arm around her waist, toward the overhanging roof of one of the concessions.

She let him lead her that far and then pushed him away. His shirt felt soggy, and she could almost feel the coldness of his flesh beneath the wet cloth.

"Don't touch me!" He still had the knife, but she felt sure he didn't intend to use it. At least not now.

He lifted his hands, palms outward. "I don't mean you any harm, Cara."

"Right! That's why you've been following me, hanging out where I work..." *Cara?* "How do you know my name?"

"I overheard someone call you by name."

She didn't believe him, not for a minute. He'd been too present, too much *there*. He'd been hanging around her for a purpose.

"And why would you be within earshot of me?" She didn't give him a chance to answer. "Because you're one of them." She gestured toward the Dumpster across the boardwalk. "You may not do the actual dirty work, but you sure as hell set me up for this."

He shook his head. "You're wrong. I've got nothing to do with that scum. I never meant you any harm."

"Then why did you send that killer after me?"

"I didn't! I swear to you, I had nothing to do with..." His sentence trailed away as footsteps came pounding down the lower walkway. They both turned in the direction of the sound.

Like a fury, Bill Hamlin took the three steps up to the boardwalk in one leap and flung himself at the man hovering over Cara.

The sounds of men swearing, panting and grunting superseded the sound of the rain.

"Be careful, Bill, please!" Cara cried out, running around the two grappling figures, trying to see how she could help Bill. The two men were equally matched in height and weight. In the rain, she could tell them apart only by their garb—Bill's plastic rain jacket and the other man's stylish trench coat. They fell to the deck, still pummeling one another and grunting epithets.

Cara looked around for a weapon.

That was when she noticed that the small man, her would-be murderer, had disappeared from beside the Dumpster.

"He's gone," she screamed, furious that he'd escaped the law, and then horrified by the realization that he was free to come after her again.

Frustration filled her lungs with power, and she screeched again, shocking the two brawling men into a momentary truce.

"Who's gone?" Bill demanded, holding back the punch that had been aimed at his opponent's face. His other hand had a stranglehold on the man's collar.

"The other guy. The one who was trying to kill me." It had taken long enough, but all of a sudden she recognized the truth; the tall man wasn't a killer, hadn't meant her any real harm, had tried to help her.

Bill seemed only to hear the word *kill*. With a roar of rage, he let go, and his fist landed with painful accuracy on the other man's eye.

"We've got this one!" Bill yelled, drawing back his arm again.

The man's shout of pain mingled with Cara's scream at Bill. "Bill, stop! He was protecting me!" She lunged at Bill, grabbing his arm, ordering him again to leave the man alone.

It took a moment for her words to sink in.

By the time the two men untangled themselves and fell back on the slippery deck, it was clear, even with their faces obscured by rain, that they'd been evenly matched and that each had given as good as he got.

"What's going on here?" Bill demanded as he staggered to his feet. "Cara, who is this guy, and who was the other guy, and what did you mean about someone trying to kill you?"

The physical circumstances of their plight struck Cara with unexpected force. She was cold, wet, tired, and aching all over. And those were only the physical symptoms. She was in no condition to deal with her emotions. She decided she wanted to be a whole lot more comfortable before she let go of those.

"I'm not saying another word until I've had a hot shower and gotten into some dry clothes," she said, forcing herself away from the wooden rail with a visible shiver. She started up the wooden walkway. "I'm going home. You guys can do whatever you want," she tossed over her shoulder.

She heard them stumbling around behind her, heard Bill say, "…coming with us until we straighten this out." Then she heard the other man's grunt of acquiescence, heard them fall into step a few feet behind her.

Chapter Twelve

The three of them sat around the kitchen table, nursing cups of hot coffee, trying to make sense of the night's events.

By the time Cara finished telling her version, Bill was up and pacing back and forth, and she had slumped back on her spine, drained from reliving the horrific experience.

"Now you," Bill growled at Gordon Lefebre. "And I want to hear everything."

Lefebre removed the towel filled with ice cubes from his left eye and nodded. He was wearing a T-shirt and a pair of Bill's sweats and had a dry towel draped around his neck for added warmth. The other two were similarly attired. Little had been said until they gathered in the kitchen and he formally introduced himself. Even then, Cara had insisted they wait until the coffee was done and they were seated at the table before they talked.

The couple had worked together to prepare and serve the coffee, and as he watched them work in silent tandem, Lefebre realized that they'd already established a considerable bond.

It should have freed him from his obsession with Cara—but it hadn't.

Lefebre began his own tale, explaining his presence in their lives. When he finished, there was a heavy silence while the other two tried to make sense of what he'd told them.

Finally Bill said, "Are you telling us you don't know who hired you?"

"I swear." Lefebre lifted his right hand as if he were truly giving an oath.

Bill nodded. That wasn't really so hard to believe. Alvaretti wasn't apt to tip his hand to a mere hireling, especially if this guy was only meant to find Bill and then set him up for the hired gun.

"I still don't understand why he'd come after me," Cara said, shaking her head. "I'm not the one he's after."

"He? He who?" Lefebre demanded, looking from one to the other. "You know the guy who hired me?"

Bill nodded. "We know who he works for."

"And that would be—?"

Bill studied Gordon Lefebre's face, trying to decide how much he could trust the man. He shrugged. What the hell? If Lefebre was lying, nothing Bill would tell him would come as a surprise. And if he was telling the truth, maybe there was some way he could help.

"Franco Alvaretti."

It appeared to take Lefebre a moment to recognize the name. When he did, he blanched, his face growing taut with shock.

"You think I was hired by the mob?" he gasped.

Bill nodded, ignoring Cara's gasp and the stunned expression on her face. This was not the time to fill Cara in on the details. The look he exchanged with her said that she clearly understood that.

"Jeez." Lefebre looked from one to the other. Suddenly his talk with his client that afternoon struck him with painful force. "My God! They're on their way here."

"What do you mean?"

"He ordered me off the case today, said they had it under control from their end now. They've got this address. They know where you work."

Bill leaped to his feet, his hands clenched in fists. "You bastard!" he shouted.

"Bill, please." Cara grabbed his arm, in case he was about to start another fight. "Mr. Lefebre didn't know who he was working for."

Bill looked around, his features taut with panic. "We've got to get out of here, Cara," he muttered. Then he grabbed her arm. "Come on, love, there's no time to waste. Let's just get going."

"What about me?" Lefebre stood up, his hands held out in submission. "I could maybe help."

Bill hesitated. No sense leaving the guy behind to help the enemy. "Turn off the pot," he called over his shoulder, "and come in here and pack for me while I scan the neighborhood, make sure we're not already in the line of fire."

Bill hurried out the front door and cautiously approached his car. So far, so good. No sign of anyone who didn't belong on the street.

He got in and drove slowly, looking up and down side streets. On one street he saw a parked car with the silhouette of a person behind the wheel. He drove past, his heart thumping erratically. It was a woman with a short haircut, a baby in a car seat beside her. The baby began to squall as the woman bent to lift it out of the car seat. She looked over at Bill as his car slowly passed hers, then shrugged and smiled. He watched in the rearview mirror and saw that she got out and went up to the house in front of which she was parked.

He did a fifteen-minute sweep, carefully covering a three-block radius, and then returned to the house, satisfied that they were unwatched for the moment.

"Hurry up," he ordered as he herded them out to the car. It was safe now, but he had no idea how long it would stay that way.

"Where are you staying?" he asked Lefebre after they'd moved out onto the street.

Lefebre told him, and suggested a shortcut to the motel.

"Do you know where we're going?" Cara asked as they waited in the motel parking lot for Lefebre. She sounded cheerful, as if they were embarking on a holiday.

Bill swallowed and put his face in his hands, rubbing his forehead with his fingertips. "I don't know." He sighed heavily, exhaustion overwhelming him.

He heard a door slam and looked up to see Lefebre starting down the outside steps from the second floor, a suitcase in one hand, a briefcase in the other.

All at once, the bleakness of his situation caught up to him. Here he was, running for his life, and he was taking on more and more responsibility. Not just Cara now, but Lefebre, as well. If he had any sense, wouldn't he dump them and just go as deep underground as he could? He had enough money to last him quite a while without working, if he lived frugally.

Only he was pretty sure now that he couldn't stand being underground. He'd learned that much about himself from the way he'd taken to playing the marriage game with Cara. It wasn't all about loving her, though God knew that was substantial all by itself; no, it was also about doing a job every day, shopping for groceries, doing odd jobs around the house. In other words, living like everyone else. He was good at that. Strangely, it made him realize how wrong he'd been in his career choice. After all, being an agent wasn't that much different from living underground. You still had to give up all the real things and live a make-believe life that really had no rewards beyond the job itself.

He pushed the trunk button inside the glove compartment as Lefebre approached the car. The man shoved his cases inside, lowered the lid and got in the back seat behind Cara.

"You've got a plan?" he asked Bill, leaning forward with his arms resting on the back of the front seat, between Bill and Cara.

"Not really," Bill said, shaking his head, his gaze going back and forth between the rearview mirror and the road ahead. "But I figured we'd go to San Francisco, via a circuitous route. Hopefully, by the time we get there, one of us will have come up with a workable idea."

They were silent for the next few miles. Cara could feel Bill's tension as he kept checking the rearview mirror. She turned sideways in her seat and looked over her left shoulder as often as he looked up. Frequently he would take unexpected turns off the highway and drive aimlessly before returning to the major route. She had a million questions running through her mind regarding Bill's connection with the mob. Instinctively she knew that this was not the time—especially with Lefebre in the car—to discuss it. Instead, she decided to lighten the mood.

"Let's play the movie game," she suggested. She turned to include Lefebre. "You too, Gordon."

But it was soon clear that Lefebre was no movie buff, though he enjoyed their knowledge and their special banter back and forth. When Bill did imitations of famous male actors and Cara quoted passages from major films, he whistled and applauded, making a marvelous one-man audience.

The game fizzled out after they'd been driving a couple of hours.

"Don't you think we got away safe?" Cara asked when they arrived at the outskirts of Daly City. She sounded tired.

Bill glanced over and saw dark circles forming beneath her eyes, giving the tender skin there a mauve cast. Lefebre had been quiet for quite some time now. Bill guessed the man was dozing.

He looked at the clock on the dash and checked it against his watch. A drive that should have taken less than an hour had taken three—a nerve-racking, tense three hours. He recognized his own exhaustion in the sore tension in the muscles of shoulder and neck.

He forced a teasing grin. "I'll trade you, a giant hamburger with all the French fries you can eat for a neck massage." He kept his voice low so that the man in the back seat wouldn't hear him.

Despite her fatigue, her smile was flirtatious. "I can stop at just one French fry. Can you stop at a neck massage?"

Bill chuckled. "Yeah, right. You eat just one French fry? I think not!"

Her fingers on the back of his neck were a silken surprise. Bill shivered and scrunched his neck against the onslaught of erotic pleasure. "Not while I'm driving," he warned, the hoarseness of his voice diminishing the authoritative quality of his words.

Cara laughed, but she withdrew her hand and leaned forward to peer through the windshield. "There's a café sign up ahead on my side."

"Okay," Bill said, though he preferred the idea of stopping in the heart of the city, where there was more to distract attention from their car.

He needed a bigger city, a larger population, anonymity. Something to close in around him. His back felt strangely exposed, vulnerable.

Lefebre sat up just then and suggested they park in back, off the main street.

"Right," Bill agreed. "You two get out here, and I'll park in back."

Cara went right to the door of the restaurant but Lefebre leaned back into the car and whispered, "Bill, do a couple of blocks before you park. I'm not sure, but I think there's a blue Honda on your tail."

So the man hadn't been sleeping. Maybe he was going to be more help than Bill had anticipated. Bill pulled away from the curb and turned the corner. He went around the block and parked facing the main drag, one block up from the café. Sure enough, a blue Honda came by, slowly, the driver leaning forward to peer through the windshield, as though looking for someone or something. The guy was wearing glasses that glinted in the illumination from the overhead street lamps. Bill watched as the Honda reached the end of the street and then picked up speed, merging with the highway traffic.

They had to get off this main strip before the Honda realized he'd lost them and backtracked, looking for them.

He pulled up in front of the café and honked the horn desperately.

He was glad to see Cara and Lefebre come rushing out without wasting a minute. They jumped into the car, no questions asked, no fanfare.

"We need to get off the main street," Bill said.

"You wouldn't have liked the menu anyway, honey," Cara said. "It was all fried food and cholesterol. I'd have been surprised if they had a lettuce leaf for a sandwich."

Bill's hands were shaking on the wheel as he turned the corner. He pulled over to the curb and turned to address Lefebre. "Excuse us a minute, pal."

He took Cara into his arms and bent his head to her shoulder, holding on to her as if his life depended on it.

"What's wrong, Bill?" Cara whispered, fear beating wildly in her chest.

"Nothing. I just needed to hold you for a minute."

He couldn't tell her that it was the very first time she'd ever called him by an affectionate term, that the domestic sound of it, and her concern for his diet preferences, had suddenly struck a chord in him that brought the fragility of their situation home to him as nothing had before.

What if it boiled down to having to live without her in order to go on living? And how had he let things get so out of hand that now he didn't even want to go on living if he couldn't have her with him?

But tonight had proved he had no choice. They'd come after Cara. She was in mortal danger, all because of him.

He gently moved her away from him.

"Cara, are you sure that guy in the park wasn't a mugger or a rapist, someone who just spotted a woman alone and decided to take advantage?" He knew he was clutching at straws, but desperate situations made desperate men.

Cara thought about it, her eyes wide with dread at the prospect. She made a gesture of denial. "No. He said...he said I was worth more than the contents of my purse, and he said if I...if I screamed, it would make an ordinary job more interesting."

"Those were his exact words?"

Cara nodded. "I'm pretty sure. Yes. Almost word for word, I think."

Bill stared out the windshield, his fingers curling and uncurling around the steering wheel as he tried to stay focused.

Something was setting off alarm bells in the farther reaches of his mind, something that should have been a major clue. He wrestled with the words Cara had quoted, trying to find the elusive truth behind the words.

But he was too tired and, now that he thought about it, very hungry. He couldn't recall having eaten at all in the past couple of days, and he definitely hadn't had much sleep.

He turned to face Lefebre. "How about we look for a place off the beaten track and then, after we eat, we find a motel and grab a few hours of shut-eye?"

"Sounds like a plan to me," Lefebre agreed. "And anytime you want me to take over the wheel, let me know."

Bill shook his head and gave the man a tired grin. "I don't know, you ride shotgun pretty well. I think I'll just let you continue to play lookout."

They passed two motels with No Vacancy signs.

"Strange," Cara commented. "There aren't many cars in the lot."

"Some lazy night clerk—or the owner himself—doesn't want to be awakened by a drop-in customer," Lefebre said.

They were just passing the second place when Lefebre called out, "Hey, Bill, I think that's the same blue Honda back there."

Bill made a U-turn and went back to check it out. It was parked in front of the last room in the row, its tail end facing the highway. He couldn't be sure it was the same car, and the license plate indicated it was a rental. Still, it was enough to send Bill in another direction.

They were only forty minutes from the heart of San Francisco. On impulse, Bill decided to go right on into the city and look for lodging there.

When they pulled up under the porte cochere of the very posh Hotel Fairmount, Cara and Lefebre began to laugh in unison.

Bill gave them a quelling look of disdain. "Would you look for us in the most prominent, most expensive hotel in the city?"

"He's got a point," Lefebre said, sobering. "And personally, this is my kind of habitat."

"Good. Then you won't mind whipping out a credit card and booking us rooms," Bill said, pushing the trunk button. "Places like this find cash-paying guests very suspicious."

The lobby was quietly elegant, and their room even more so. But Cara and Bill didn't waste much time reveling in their luxurious surroundings. Bill just barely had time to lock the door and draw the drapes before Cara hurled herself at him and began to pull his shirt from the waistband of his jeans.

The king-size bed occupied much of the room. They fell onto it the minute the last scrap of clothing had been stripped away and tossed willy-nilly over a shoulder.

An hour later, they lay side by side, holding hands, drifting toward sleep.

"We'll get up before morning and continue on," Bill said, drowsily.

"Mm-hmm... Right." Cara sighed deeply, happily, and turned over to curl up along the naked length of her lover. He let go of her hand and slipped his arm under her body to hold her close.

"What do you think of Gordon?" Cara asked, snuggling into his side.

Bill stroked curls away from her forehead as he pondered his answer. "He's certainly not typical."

"Of what?"

"Of Alvaretti's people."

"Bill, you promised you'd tell me about yourself. I assume it has something to do with Alvaretti. Can you tell me now?"

Bill let go of her and turned onto his back, tucking his hands behind his head, staring up at the ceiling.

Cara propped an extra pillow under her cheek and waited.

"As you obviously know by now, I'm hiding from Alvaretti."

"Yes, but why?" She lifted her head off the pillow, her eyes wide with alarm. "You weren't in the mob, were you?"

Bill sighed. "Yes and no." He turned so that he was facing her. "I'm... I *was* a special agent with the Justice Department. I was assigned to use my accounting skills to penetrate Alvaretti's bookkeeping system. Once I'd done that and turned the evidence over to my people, they were able to put Alvaretti out of commission and into the slammer, but then that left me vulnerable to Alvaretti's revenge."

"You were an agent? Like in the FBI?" Cara's voice was heavy with awe.

Bill smiled wryly. "Don't be too impressed. The minute my cover was blown, I was out of a job."

"It's just that I never thought when I was cramming for those accounting exams that it could lead to such an adventurous career."

"Yeah, well, if anyone ever offers you the job, just remember that even bookkeeping can be hazardous to your health."

"If Alvaretti's in jail, how can he hurt you?"

Bill blinked and then squinted at Cara, as if seeing her for the first time. "Are you kidding? Do you really think changing his place of operation can stop someone like Franco Alvaretti? He's head of the mob, for Christ sake, Cara."

"You don't need to snap at me, Bill Hamlin! I think most *normal* citizens would believe that putting a guy in jail is a sure way to stop his criminal activities. And furthermore, I don't appreciate..."

She stopped, her face registering a new thought. "Is Bill Hamlin your real name?"

Bill grinned and put out his hand. "Bill Spencer, at your service, ma'am."

Cara stared at her lover. "It suits you," she said finally, in a small, hollow voice.

"Cara?" Bill sat up and pulled her up to face him. "What's wrong, love?"

Cara shook her head. "Nothing. It's just difficult to find out, after we've been so intimate, that I didn't even know your name," she remarked shyly.

Bill chuckled and lifted her chin so that she had to meet his eyes. "Haven't you ever heard of love with the perfect stranger?"

That restored her, as he'd known it would. She punched him in the stomach and pushed him away.

"Perfect, indeed! And I don't think anything one does with a stranger, perfect or otherwise, could be deemed love!"

Bill rolled away from the threat of another punch, laughing, and then grabbed her arms and pulled her up against his chest.

"Give me a kiss, my love, and I'll prove we're far from strangers."

The kiss made her dizzy, almost made her forget the topic of conversation that had preceded the intimacy.

Her lips were wet and her eyes shiny when she pulled away. "We're not through talking yet, Bi— What do I call you now?"

"Bill." Bill sobered. "That was one of the reasons I didn't want you to know the truth. It's very difficult to juggle too much information, too many lies. I'm going to use Bill Hamlin as long as I can. After that, I may have to resort to another pseudonym, and you'll have to learn that one and not make any mistakes."

Cara nodded, suddenly frightened again. This was serious business. They could avoid looking at the danger by making love, pretending to be a normal couple, laughing and joking about things, but apparently Bill knew something about the prison system that she didn't, and his fear of Alvaretti was very real.

"Where are we going? Where do you think we'll be safe?"

"Cara, there's something I never told you. When I thought you were a plant, back in Utah, I went to your room. I . . ." He felt his face grow warm with embarrassment. "I read your journal. I know why you left home."

It was Cara's turn to blush. "You didn't think. . ." She could hardly meet Bill's eyes, though she forced herself to do so. Her chin came up defiantly. If he thought she'd encouraged Doug Harvard...

Bill grabbed her and held her tight. "Cara, I didn't think for a minute that it was in any way your fault," he said, knowing that victims often took on undeserved guilt.

Cara's sigh trembled against Bill's chest. "I didn't know what else to do. I had to get away from there."

"I know, love." He pulled away from her and looked deep into her eyes. "I've been thinking, though, that maybe it's time for you to go home and face him. After all, keeping quiet is only putting your mother at risk. If you're out of the picture, who's going to make her see what a sleaze the guy is?"

Hope lit up her face. "Do you think there's a way to do it so she doesn't resent me, or even hate me?"

He couldn't imagine anyone hating her, and he told her so.

"She was so lonely after Dad died, it was hard for her to even relate to me in her grief," Cara told him. "She shut me out while she was going through that, and then, when she met Doug, she acted as if she'd been given a second chance at happiness. I didn't want to be the one to rob her of that."

Bill nodded. "I see where you're coming from. But how happy is she going to be with a guy who'd hit on her own daughter? And with you gone, don't you think he'll find some other young thing to play with?"

He poured water from the bedside carafe as Cara mulled that over. He handed her the glass.

Cara drank and then handed the glass back to him. "You're right, I should go back." She grabbed his arm. "But what about you? What about us?"

Bill drained the glass and set it down on the tray, his back to Cara. "I'll go with you."

There was a momentary silence, and then Cara squealed as his words sank in. "You'll go home with me? You really will? Oh, Bill, that's terrific!"

"Shh," Bill ordered, laughing as he turned back to see the look of excitement and pleasure in her face. "Not so loud. You'll get us kicked out, and it's..." He glanced at his watch and groaned. "It's four o'clock in the morning. We've got to get some sleep."

"We've got to make plans."

Bill slipped under the sheet and pulled her down beside him. "In the morning, love. We need some rest before we move on, and we don't have much time to squander here in San Francisco."

"All right, hon, we'll make plans in the morning," Cara whispered, snuggling into the crook of his arm.

They were each aware of a renewed, if less frantic, yearning of flesh for flesh. But fatigue won out in the end.

DOWN THE HALL, Lefebre lay awake in his bed, examining the way his feelings toward Cara had changed. Now he was obsessed by them as a couple. You couldn't be around them ten minutes, he thought, without becoming aware of the intense chemistry between them. Not necessarily a physical thing, or at least not that alone. They *felt right together.* They had an air of continuity, as if they had been together forever and would continue to be, no matter what obstacles were thrown in their path. It was almost as if their lives were a base reality and everyone and everything around them were just props for their adventure.

And he, Gordo, was one of those props, he supposed. Whatever happened to them, they'd go on, and he'd soon be just a dim memory, if that much.

He turned on his side and stared at the wall. Maybe that wasn't a fair analysis of the situation. Maybe it was just that because they had each other, Bill and Cara didn't need anyone else.

He started to doze, but his mind was too revved up to allow him sleep. Like a movie reel playing across the screen of his memory, he began to review fragments of conversation, images of events.

The little punk attacking Cara... Franco Alvaretti... Bill running from the mob... Cara attacked by a hit man sent out by Alvaretti... The client...

Something off kilter there, pieces that didn't quite fit. But he couldn't slow his thoughts long enough to sort things out. And then they slowed down so completely that his brain felt sluggish and he drifted into sleep.

THE TRIO met for breakfast in the hotel dining room after Bill called Lefebre to suggest they eat and then head out.

"You've got a plan," Lefebre noted, seeing the look on Bill's face.

"Yeah. We're going back east. Cara has business to settle with her mother, and I think that part of the country will be safe for me, at least for a while."

Lefebre popped a piece of croissant into his mouth and pretended indifference. "Mind if I tag along?"

Bill looked surprised. "Don't you have a business to run, a home to go to?"

Lefebre shrugged. "I work for myself, and I made enough on this job to hold me for a while. And no, I don't have a home in the usual sense of the word. Just an apartment that never seems to notice if I'm in it or not.''

Now Cara looked surprised. Such an attractive, charming, obviously intelligent man, with no family? And he wasn't young. She suspected he was close to her mother's age, though he had a slim figure and there was very little gray in his hair. Maybe it was the eyes that betrayed age, something in the creases at the corners, or that glint that spoke of too many things seen and felt.

''What happened to your family, Gordon?'' she asked, sure that somewhere in his history there had been people who cared for him.

''It's a long story'' was all Lefebre said, reaching for his orange juice. It was enough to hinder any further questions.

There had been a time when he might have fantasized about telling Cara the story of his life, but that time had passed, if indeed it had ever really existed. What he wanted now was to see the two of them settled, safe. He wanted to be part of making that happen, if he could.

''So what's the agenda, Bill—and listen, why don't you call me Gordon? I think we've gone past formality, don't you?''

Bill put down his toast, swallowed, wiped his hand on his napkin and held it across the table. ''Yeah, I agree.'' They shook hands.

''Let's start with you repeating everything you reported about us to your client.''

''Just your address and place of employment,'' Lefebre assured Bill as he picked up his fork.

''Not a description of our car or the plate numbers?''

''No, that never came up.''

"Okay. But I think we should unload the car anyway, given that possible encounter with the blue Honda. We'll get another and head out right away."

"We're going to drive back east?" Lefebre asked.

"I think that's safest, don't you? It's too easy to trace people on public transportation."

Lefebre agreed. That was how he'd caught up with them in the first place.

Again a bothersome thought nagged at his mind, but just then the waiter brought the bill and he was distracted by the business of getting out his credit card.

"I assume I'm not financing the whole trip, buddy?" he joked.

"Gee, Gordon, I thought that's why you wanted to join us," Bill said. He stood up and took a couple of bills out of his pocket, tossing them on the table in front of Lefebre. "That'll take care of our rooms and breakfast," he said. "You can pick up the tab for lunch."

It took most of the morning to buy another car. Since a trade-in would be too risky as far as blowing their cover, Lefebre dropped Bill a block from a used-car lot, and he and Cara went to the airport, where he parked the old car in long-term parking. They took a cab back to the city and waited for Bill down at the wharf, where they could get lost in the rash of tourists.

Bill drove up in a gray Oldsmobile Cutlass that was less than two years old and showed no signs of wear, except for a hole in the dash where the radio had been removed. It had cost a nice chunk of his nest egg, but if he got lucky and didn't have to ditch it, too, it would prove worth the cost. A man on the run needed reliable transportation.

Cara bought them all shrimp cocktail and sourdough bread from kiosks on the wharf, and they lunched in the car as they started the trip cross-country.

Chapter Thirteen

The house was a surprise to Bill.

"It's a damned mansion!"

In the back seat Lefebre chuckled. "I could live with it."

Cara looked from one to the other and then leaned forward to stare past Bill at the home where she'd grown up.

"I guess it is," she said, rather meekly. "I just never thought of it that way. To me it was just a house, like any other, only maybe a little bigger."

She felt her insides quivering with excitement at seeing her home again, knowing her mother was just inside.

"Mm-hmm...and to me, a gold nugget is just a dirty hunk of metal you dig out of the ground," Lefebre said, teasingly.

They were parked across the street, looking over at a stone edifice with iron gates that opened onto an extra-wide drive, curved past a front portico and then came out at a second set of gates. The house and grounds took up half the block. The houses on either side, though large in their own right, seemed insignificant beside it. Huge old trees towered along the boulevard.

"Are you ready?" Bill asked Cara.

Cara took a deep breath and exhaled it on a hefty sigh. "As I'll ever be. But I've decided to do it a little differently."

"Differently? How? Why can't you stick to the plan?" Bill knew his irritation was based largely on the fact that he would soon be meeting Cara's mother, and he was already feeling intimidated just from the sight of the Dunlap homestead.

"There's a little side gate along the fence on this side of the house. It's usually left unlocked. There are French doors leading into the breakfast room on that side of the house. It's my mother's favorite room—an office of sorts. If she's home, she's more apt to be there at this hour than anywhere else in the house. If I can get her attention and get her outside, I can to talk to her alone before I have to deal with Doug."

Dusk was just beginning to cast shadows over the street, though it was already nine o'clock in the evening. Cara remembered her father used to call it the "gloaming" and that it had been his favorite time of day, especially on a summer night like this. Remembering made her throat ache a little—and strengthened her resolve to confront her mother and, consequently, Doug Harvard.

"Let's wait a little," she told Bill. "Just until it gets a little darker, so Doug doesn't see me approaching the house."

"Cara, you're going to have to face Harvard sooner or later, and you're going to have us with you."

Cara shook her head. "Not at first. You promised. I want some time alone with my mother, so I can tell her what a sleaze her boyfriend is in private." She put her hand on Bill's arm and half turned in her seat to include Lefebre. "You understand, don't you? I'm afraid my mother would not appreciate being humiliated in front of strangers.''

Bill could understand that, especially now that the reality of the Dunlap family's social position was becoming evident.

Lefebre cleared his throat. "If your mother's anything like you, Cara, she's going to take it like a trouper."

"Thanks, Gordon," Cara said, smiling at their new friend.

"Well," Lefebre said, sliding toward the door, "I guess I'll go for a walk and have a smoke while we're waiting for it to get dark."

The minute they were alone, Cara slid over to curl up under Bill's arm. She kissed his cheek and then rubbed lipstick off with her fingertips. "Bill, does it feel safe here?"

Bill thought about the drive up through the New England countryside. "Yeah, it does," he said. "I didn't really think about it before you asked, but yes, it feels pretty good." He frowned then and added, "But I'm not sure how long it will be safe, Cara. I may have to leave here, as well."

"We."

"What?"

"*We* may have to leave."

She didn't notice Bill's lack of response.

"Bill, how do you think they tracked you down in Utah? Did Gordon ever say?"

Bill shook his head, frustration etched across his brow. "I don't know. Gordon only knows that his client called and told him to fly out to Utah and catch up with the bus at Salt Lake City. I've been driving myself batty trying to retrace my steps, to figure out where I went wrong, where I left a clue. It had to be that Alvaretti got lucky, and one of his people discovered me by accident. His people are everywhere across the country— Jeez, the people we worked for or our landlord or any of the restaurant owners where we ate our meals...even the bus driver...any of 'em could have been mob-related."

He reached over and took Cara's hand, holding it securely in both of his. "Let's change the subject for now, okay?"

Cara looked surprised. "Why?"

Bill cleared his throat and rubbed the back of her hand with his thumb. "It's just that you're about to be reunited with your mother, and we're in a totally different situation now. We can't change what happened back in Santa Cruz, so let's just enjoy the present and pretend there is no past or future."

Cara laughed and nuzzled Bill's neck. "No future? No way. I've already picked out names for our first four babies."

Bill felt alarm shoot through him like a bolt of lightning. Hadn't he gotten through to her, made her understand that if Alvaretti's people found him they were both in grave danger? There weren't going to be any babies, or anything else that required permanence, roots.

He was going to be on the run for the rest of his life.

It had been weeks since he'd faced that fact head-on. He'd let his relationship with Cara, their love for each other, delude him into pretending they could somehow make it together. But that was a false hope; once he got Cara settled here and helped get rid of Harvard, he was going to have to think about moving on.

He and Lefebre had discussed that over beers one evening in one of the motel bars where they'd stopped for the night. Cara had turned in early, fatigued from the long day's drive.

"Do you see yourself settling down in Greensville?" had been Lefebre's opening gambit.

"I don't see that happening," Bill had admitted. "At least not in the way you mean. I figure if they could catch up with me in Utah, after the pains I went through to cover my tracks, it's only a matter of time before they trace me to Massachusetts. How much time is the only thing in question."

Lefebre had nodded his understanding and then said, "I'm going to miss the two of you. I don't suppose you'd consider joining forces with me in my little agency? I get some jobs that call for more than one guy."

Bill had shaken his head. "Have you thought about the fact that if Alvaretti finds out we've teamed up, he's going to think of you as having betrayed him?"

"Hell, I gave him what he bought and paid for. Why should I owe him loyalty, as well?"

"Because that's how warped his thinking is. I figure, after Cara and her mother come to an understanding, and you and I make sure Harvard hits the road when Mrs. Dunlap gives him the boot, you should go back to your own life—while you still have one."

Now that he looked back on it, it seemed that Lefebre had agreed only rather reluctantly.

He lifted his arm from around Cara and nodded toward the windshield. "It's getting dark, Cara. Do you think you can make it to the side gate now without being seen?"

Cara felt nervousness pervading her being, but she braced herself, careful not to let Bill sense her uneasiness. "Okay, hon, I'm gone." She put her hand on the door handle.

"Let's have a kiss for luck, love," Bill said, and Cara willingly turned to him again. The embrace was tender, though brief.

Within seconds of that kiss, Cara found herself on the sidewalk about to cross in front of the car. In the near dark, she could just make out the glowing ember of Gordon's cigarette, up the street. He was walking toward her, passing in front of the Marquette house.

If the Marquettes still live there. Now where had that thought come from? After all, she'd only been gone from home about two months. Yet it felt as if everything in the neighborhood could have changed in her absence.

Maybe because only her weeks with Bill held any reality for her now. Bill was her home now; not Greensville, and not Dunlap House.

Still, before she cut her ties with Greensville once and for all, she had to free her mother. *And the truth shall set you free,* she thought.

The side gate was unlocked, as she had anticipated. It creaked slightly, and she waited, holding her breath, to see if anyone inside the house would hear it and come to a window.

After a few minutes, she determined that it was safe and slipped into the side garden, keeping to the stone path, which was bordered by rosebushes.

There were two sets of French doors, the first opening out of the library. Her destination was the next set.

She didn't realize she'd been holding her breath until she came abreast of the library and, peering in, saw Doug Harvard in a wing chair across the room, apparently dozing, with a newspaper open across his lap.

She pulled back against the wall of the house, her heart pounding, her limbs shaking.

Several minutes went by before she was calm enough to risk another peek into the room to satisfy herself that Doug was indeed asleep.

He appeared not to have moved an iota. She took another breath and crept past the glass doors, walking on tiptoe through the grass.

Her heart sank when she saw that the breakfast room was empty. But a brass table lamp was lit and, knowing her mother's frugal tendency to save pennies wherever she could, Cara suspected her mother had been there not long ago and had every intention of returning—hopefully momentarily.

Now she faced a new dilemma. Should she enter the room and wait for her mother, taking a chance that her mother would cry out in surprise, alerting the servants and Doug Harvard? Or should she stay out here and tap gently on the window to get her mother's attention?

The sight of her mother entering the room cast out her indecision. With a smile on her face, her mother's name on her lips, Cara reached for the handle of the door.

Her hand had only just touched metal when she felt the gun in her back and heard Doug Harvard's dreaded voice in her ear.

BILL'S FINGERS tapped on the edge of the wheel, and he whistled tunelessly under his breath. Beside him, Lefebre's foot jiggled nervously, and every few minutes he exhaled a heavy sigh.

"Long time," Lefebre said finally.

They both looked over toward the house.

"They had a lot to talk about," Bill said.

Another silence, punctuated by Bill's fingers drumming and Lefebre's sighs.

"You suppose she's inside?"

Bill hadn't thought about that. He'd been busy trying to guess Mrs. Dunlap's response to Cara's accusations against Harvard.

"I don't know."

Lefebre cleared his throat. "How much do you know about this Harvard?"

Bill's fingers closed around the wheel. "Other than the fact that he hit on Cara and made her life hell?"

"Yeah. I mean, what did she tell you about who he is, his background and so forth."

"*Nada.*" Bill shook his head. "You think there's some sort of history?"

Lefebre shrugged. "Could be."

Bill looked over at the house again. He pushed the button that lowered his window and listened. No sound to alarm him. From up the street he could hear a dog barking, but apart from that, the street was quiet.

The look he slanted at the other man was both thoughtful and ominous. "We'll give her ten more minutes and then we go in."

"MOVE BACK QUIETLY and don't make a sound," Harvard warned, jabbing the gun into her side for emphasis.

Cara obeyed and felt herself being pushed back along the side of the house.

When they came to the library doors, Harvard pushed her inside, and she heard the key turning in the lock behind her. "Get over there," Harvard ordered, shoving her toward the desk.

"What are you doing?" Cara demanded. "You aren't going to get away with this." Should she tell him about Bill and Lefebre, that she hadn't come alone? No. Why warn him? They were her ace in the hole.

"I don't think you're in any position to challenge me, dear Cara," Harvard said. He kept the gun on her and looked around for something with which to tie her up. His glance fell on the ties that held back the heavy linen drapes. He snatched a pair off the nearest window and ordered Cara to put her hands behind her.

"Why are you doing this, Doug? I only came back to see my mother. I didn't plan to stay."

"Right. And that's why you were sneaking in the back way instead of coming to the front door."

She had no answer to that. She tried appealing to his sense of self-preservation. "I don't know what you're thinking, Doug, but how do you suppose the law is going to view your waving a gun at me and tying me up?"

Harvard laughed and bent to tie her ankles. He hesitated only a moment, his hand hovering over her calf. He shook his head and applied himself to the business of fastening her legs with the drapery tie.

"You don't seem to get the picture, Cara. The law isn't going to be involved until long after the fact. By that time, there won't be any evidence to connect me to you."

"What about Mom?" Cara heard the quiver in her voice and hoped Harvard wouldn't interpret it as fear. The last thing she wanted was for him to know exactly how scared she was. Pretty silly thinking, Cara, she told herself, when you're being tied up at gunpoint.

"Exactly," Harvard said. "What *about* Mom?" He tested the knot and nodded with satisfaction before getting to his feet. "Well, it's like this, my beauty—since you've been away, Mom has been a naughty girl, drinking too much and even taking up smoking."

His grin was a wolf's leer. "Mom is going to learn that those vices can be hazardous to one's health." He laughed again, and Cara realized he was actually enjoying this.

"Unfortunately, your mother's bad habits are going to affect everyone else in the house, as well. Now isn't that a shame?"

He started toward the door, waving the gun. "Don't go away, Cara," he called out in a singsong voice. "I'll be back for you as soon as I finish with your mother."

Cara wondered where Mrs. Malcom, the housekeeper, was. And what about Joe, the gardener? The maid didn't live in, so she'd be gone for the day, but surely the other two would hear her if she screamed.

She opened her mouth to do just that and realized she'd only incur Harvard's wrath. He'd gag her, and then she wouldn't be able to let Bill and Gordon know where she was when they came looking for her.

And they would. When she didn't come back out to the car to get them after a reasonable amount of time, they'd know something was wrong and they'd storm the castle, as it were.

And then Doug would shoot them.

Her heart sank. They were in just as much danger as she and her mother. They would come to the door and ring the bell politely, not knowing Doug had a gun. When they asked for her, he'd know they were her backup, and he'd kill them, too.

Kill. It hit her then. He meant to kill her and her mother and anyone else who got in his way. But why?

For her mother's money.

She realized then that that had been his plan all along.

Desperation stirred her to action. She began to twist and turn, attempting to free her hands from their bonds.

IN THE NEXT ROOM, Beth Dunlap Harvard was drinking the martini her husband had so kindly prepared for her. She couldn't hurt his feelings by telling him she didn't care for a drink just now. He'd been so attentive lately, bringing her drinks, lighting her cigarettes.

He held one out to her now. She took it, smiling into his eyes, afraid to say she didn't know why she'd taken up smoking again after so long. Her memory was so hazy lately. She could have sworn that Doug had urged her to take up cigarettes again, but surely that couldn't be true. Doug didn't even smoke himself.

"Thank you, darling," she said. She flinched when she heard the slight slur in her voice. "I'm afraid I'm the tiniest bit tipsy, darling," she told her husband.

Doug laughed and tipped his own glass back. "So what, darling? We're in the privacy of our own home. Why shouldn't we have a little fun?"

Because she wasn't sure this *was* fun. She'd been waking up with terrible hangovers lately, and her mouth tasted like a dirty ashtray after she'd smoked cigarettes all evening. The servants and their friends at the country club, and even some of her neighbors, had begun to look at her strangely.

Her hand shook as she emptied her glass. Doug immediately jumped forward to refill it from the pitcher he'd brought with him into the room. "Attagirl, Bethie, one more drink and we'll tippytoe upstairs and have ourselves one of our little parties."

She knew what that meant. Her reward. Physical favors in exchange for being the obedient, docile wife.

She wondered what Doug would think if she told him that she no longer enjoyed his sexual advances, that the constant drinking had dulled her senses so that she just wanted to curl up and sleep when they got into bed.

Maybe she wasn't drinking enough. Maybe if she drank a little more, she'd actually pass out when he led her to their bed. She accepted the glass he held out to her and tossed back the contents in two swallows.

THEY WERE just about to leave the car, to go over to the house to look for Cara, when a car turned the corner onto the street. It was a cab, its roof light a yellow beacon. It slowed and stopped directly alongside the Olds. Automatically Bill and Lefebre slouched down in their seats.

They heard the cab's door slam, and the sound of it pulling away.

They sat up slowly, in unison.

A man was moving quickly toward the Dunlap house.

Lefebre gasped and grabbed Bill's arm.

"That's him!"

"Who? Harvard?"

"No. That's the punk who tried to kill Cara at the boardwalk."

"Let's go!"

Bill had his hand on the door handle when Lefebre pulled him back.

"Wait!"

"For what? For him to kill Cara?"

"Don't you see what this means?"

"Yeah, the sleaze who tried to kill Cara is in there with the sleaze who drove her out of her own home in the first pla— Jee-zus!"

Lefebre nodded. "Exactly! We've been barking up the wrong tree."

"But you said you were hired by Alvaretti."

"No, I didn't. You did. I just told you I was hired by someone I'd never seen before."

"What?"

"Damn, that's the missing piece. Let's go!"

Now it was Bill's turn to hold Lefebre back. "What's going on? What just happened?"

"Don't you get it? Harvard is the guy who hired me. I'd been following you as a couple from the time I caught up with you, so I forgot my original assignment."

"Which was?"

"To follow Cara!"

By the time they got out of their respective doors, the little man from the boardwalk had already disappeared inside the Dunlap mansion.

"Have you got a gun?" Bill asked Lefebre. His friend shook his head. "I'm not licensed for weapons."

"Well, I have, and license or no, I think we're going to need it." He went to the trunk and reached for his briefcase.

"Are we going to ring the doorbell?" Lefebre asked in a whisper.

Bill closed the trunk as quietly as he could. "Uh-uh," he whispered back. "We're going to follow Cara's plan and go through that side gate."

DOUG HEARD THE DOORBELL and spun around, panic causing him to drop the martini pitcher to the carpet.

"Ooh, naughty boy," his wife said teasingly. "Malc'm's gonna scooold you."

"Stay here!"

He rushed from the room, confident that Beth was too sloshed to move on her own.

The man he spied through the curtain at the front door was Harry Wilder. Doug stuck the gun inside his shirt and opened the door.

"Harry—what the hell are you doing here?"

"Hi, Doug. We need to talk."

"Yeah? Sure, come on in." He led the way into the living room, across from the library, sparing only a quick glance at the closed door behind which Cara was incarcerated.

He was sweating, he realized, trying to juggle too much at once. But he had to get rid of Wilder.

"So, Harry, what brings you back here? I expected you to finish the job on the Coast." He gestured for Wilder to take a seat on the couch and he sat down in a club chair across from him.

"She disappeared, Doug. Like off the face of the earth. I figured she might be on her way back here, and you'd want me to finish the job."

"Hmm... I see what you mean. Too bad you couldn't do it right the first time, Harry," Doug said, getting a grip on his nerves.

"Hey, you didn't warn me she wasn't no little wuss. She was one tough bird, let me tell you, and she had help besides."

"Help? Oh, you mean the guy she was living with? You mean you couldn't take him, too?"

"You wasn't up-front with me, Doug. If you wanted 'em both rubbed, you shoulda paid me more." Wilder was whining now.

Doug stood abruptly, pulling the throw pillow from behind his back and drawing the gun with his other hand.

The pillow made a perfect silencer, reducing the sound of the shot to a loud pop. Wilder looked surprised and then panicked as he fell forward, slumping to the floor.

Harvard shoved the gun in his shirt and bent to pick up the body, tossing it over his shoulder like a sack of flour. He went out to the large front hall and looked around.

He carried the body to the closet under the stairs and unceremoniously shoved it inside.

He was sweating profusely now. He wiped his face with his shirtsleeve. Beth. Step one. He had to get her upstairs and in bed.

Step two was to deal with Cara.

THE TIE was starting to give, Cara was sure of it. She'd tried to flex her wrists when Doug was tying them, but he'd worked too fast. Still, it felt as if they were loosening. She prayed that wasn't just wishful thinking and that she'd get free in time to help her mother. Her other prayer was that Bill and Gordon wouldn't come to the house at all, that something would delay them so that Doug wouldn't kill them, as well.

She twisted the fingers of her right hand and found slack beneath one strand of the tie. It was looser!

The door burst open, and Harvard came tearing in, his face oily with sweat, his eyes glazed. "Come on," he ordered, snatching her by the arm and pulling her to her feet.

But her ankles were tied together. She couldn't walk. Harvard swore and knelt to untie them. His palms were wet and his fingers kept slipping. He repeatedly rubbed them on his pants, all the while swearing and panting with the effort.

All too soon, he had the bands free and was dragging Cara along, urging her toward the stairs in the front hall.

"Where are we going?" Cara gasped, trying to pull back.

Harvard pulled out the gun and waved it in her face. "We're going where I say we're going. Now move it!" He shoved her so hard that she stumbled and fell. He jerked her to her feet, and she felt herself being propelled upward by his hand on her back.

On the second floor, they passed the master bedroom, and Cara saw her mother stretched out on the bed, a glass in her hand. She dug her heels in and refused to go on.

"I want to see my mother."

"Your mother's tired. She needs her rest."

"Why does she have a glass in her hand?"

"She gets thirsty during the night." Harvard laughed, and the sound sent chills up Cara's back. The man was truly mad.

They rounded the bend in the hall. He pushed her into the room that had been hers all the years she'd lived in the house. For a moment, her eyes filled with tears, as she thought of how different it might have been if this had just been a homecoming visit to her mother.

He pushed her onto the bed, and Cara feared he planned to attack her sexually. But he was past that.

She had barely landed on her back when he was out the door.

She began to work again on the wrist ties, thinking she should run, but not knowing where to run to get away from the very mad Doug Harvard.

BILL AND LEFEBRE CREPT through the hall, keeping to the shadows.

They'd found the French doors open and entered the room Cara had described as a breakfast room. There had been a glass pitcher lying on the rug, and an ashtray filled with cigarette butts on a table.

Lefebre had bent and retrieved the pitcher, sniffing its interior. "Gin. Martinis I think."

They'd waited to make sure nobody was around before creeping out into the central hall. There were muted sounds from overhead, but none on the ground floor.

They came to the staircase, and Bill halted when he spied the door under the stairs. It was slightly ajar. He tiptoed over and eased the door open.

A leg fell out onto the tile floor, and Bill jumped back with a cry of fright. Lefebre clamped a hand over Bill's mouth, and they both gazed upward, wondering if Bill's shout had been heard.

After a couple moments, they relaxed and turned their attention to the body in the closet.

"That's the guy who tried to waste Cara," Lefebre whispered.

"He won't be wasting anyone else," Bill commented, unable to feel any pity for the late would-be murderer.

"Yeah, but now we know how desperate Harvard is," Lefebre reminded.

"Cripes, this place is massive," Bill lamented. "How the hell are we going to find her?"

Bill looked at Lefebre's face and saw his own fears mirrored in his friend's eyes. *If she isn't already dead.* Bill felt a stab of intense pain in his chest, as he realized they were both thinking the same horrible thought.

When Lefebre gestured toward the stairs, Bill shook his head. "We're too exposed there," he whispered. "There's bound to be servants' stairs in the back. Let's find those."

They passed through a butler's pantry and a kitchen large enough to prepare food for the town's entire school system. The stairs were on the other side of the kitchen, in a second pantry, lined with glass-fronted cabinetry that housed the mansion's supply of serving pieces.

The stairs wound upward in a circular fashion, with no mercy for the hired help who might be toting down baskets of laundry or trays of dishes. The treads were wooden, and so worn that they actually curved inward in the middle. In one or two cases, they creaked, causing Bill and Lefebre to freeze in place.

It seemed to take forever—due to their caution—to make it to the second floor.

They would have worked their way from door to door, in that same cautious way, looking for Cara, but just then a desperate scream rang out, and both men were started into action.

Chapter Fourteen

Cara's hands pulled free from the loosened ties just as the scream rent the air. She sprang to her feet, prepared to follow the sound, when suddenly the door slammed open and Harvard came running in.

She didn't think twice. The knickknack shelving was next to the bed. She snatched the big pottery bowl she'd made in art class and ran at Harvard, catching him off guard and smashing him on the head with all her might. The bowl didn't even break, but Harvard slid to the floor, the gun falling at his feet.

Cara left man and gun and ran out into the hall, almost knocking over her lover.

"Oh, my God, you're safe, you're all right!" Bill grabbed Cara, overwhelmed with emotion at finding her all right.

Cara pushed him away, crying, "Mom! Mom!" She barely acknowledged Lefebre as she fled past him, heading for her mother's room, dreading what had precipitated that scream.

It wasn't until she rounded the bend in the hall that led to her mother's suite that she smelled the smoke.

Bill's and Lefebre's footsteps were thundering behind her. "Fire!" she cried over her shoulder. "Extinguishers in the linen closet at the end of the hall!"

She herself moved forward, determined to get to her mother in time.

"Cara, wait, don't go in there!" Bill called after her. But Cara ignored him.

Smoke was already seeping from under her mother's bedroom door. When she flung it open, the smoke enveloped her, and she saw that the bed was encased in flames and that the window treatments were already curling upward in a blaze.

She screamed her mother's name, choking on smoke, tears streaming down her cheeks. Was her mother already charred in that inferno? Panic gripped her. For a moment, she was held captive by her fear. The heat in the room was daunting. She ran forward, tripping on something—something soft.

With a shout of relief, she knelt to feel the outline of her mother.

Behind her, she heard the men's shouts and the hiss and spray of the extinguishers being activated.

"The bed's a loss!" she heard Lefebre yell. "Point it at the windows!"

"Bill, help me," she called as she tried to lift her mother's limp weight. "My mother's unconscious."

He was at her side in a moment, lifting Beth Dunlap up into his capable arms.

"Let's get out of here!" Lefebre shouted. "These things aren't going to do the job!"

Smoke followed them down the stairs as they hurried to keep ahead of the blaze. They heard roaring and crackling behind them.

Cara jumped the last two steps and led the way to the double front doors. They breathed in fresh air in greedy gulps. Cara turned to make sure her mother was still alive and untouched by the fire. The older woman's face was blackened by soot, and she was clearly unconscious.

"Hospital's about three blocks from here," Cara said. "Let's get her there."

They were just getting into the car when Bill looked back. Flames were shooting from windows on the second floor, and in the distance they could hear the sound of sirens. Someone must have smelled smoke or seen flames and called in the fire.

"Where's Gordon?"

"He was right behind me," Bill said, his throat suddenly very dry.

He was about to run back for him when Lefebre came staggering out of the front door, a man's body draped over his shoulder.

Bill met him in the driveway and saw that Lefebre's burden was the corpse from the closet.

Lefebre's face was black, and his eyes were red. He grinned. "Evidence. Don't want Harvard to get away with anything."

Bill clapped his friend on the shoulder. "Good thinking, Gordo. We're on the way to the hospital with Cara's mother. What are you going to do with the...er, evidence?"

"I'll wait here for the cops. You go ahead. Nobody needs to know you were here. I'll catch up with you later."

As he hurried back to the car, it dawned on Bill that he was thanking his lucky stars for Gordon Lefebre more and more frequently these days.

CARA SAT by her mother's bed, holding the older woman's hand.

"Smoke inhalation," the doctor had said, shaking his head. "Might not have been so bad, but she'd apparently had quite a bit to drink before the fire. We couldn't even medicate her, because of the alcohol."

Cara had nodded. Harvard had told her about that. "Do you know when Mother started drinking, Dr. Zachary? I don't recall her ever having more than an occasional glass of wine."

"You're right, Cara, your mother and father were both pretty much abstainers." He looked a trifle embarrassed, and he avoided Cara's eyes. "Um . . . I'd have to say we all first noticed it after your mother married that young Harvard."

"Married?" Cara's shriek could be heard out in the corridor, where Bill paced, waiting for news of Mrs. Dunlap's condition.

He rushed to the door of the room and saw that Cara was sitting by the bed, a stricken look on her face. She waved Bill away. "It's okay, honey," she said. "Please wait outside."

When he'd gone, Cara turned back to the doctor. "I didn't know they'd actually married. When . . . when did they marry?"

Dr. Zachary patted her hand. "About a week after we heard you'd left town."

So this was her fault. If she'd stayed to fight Doug, all of this might never have happened. She swallowed hard, holding back tears of frustration, and picked up her mother's hand again.

"I've got to see to another patient, Cara, but I'll be back in a bit."

Cara was unaware of the amount of time that passed as she sat by her mother's bedside. It had been dark when they brought her in. She glanced out the window and saw light streaking the sky.

She'd spent the passing hours attempting to sort out her own responsibility in her mother's near death. Her cowardice had given Harvard all the freedom he needed to work on Beth Dunlap. On the other hand, the Dunlap women had always had what her father used to refer to as "a little too much backbone," so maybe nothing would have dissuaded her mother. It was hard to think of her mother drinking to excess, and the idea that she'd started smoking again was almost absurd. She remembered when her mother had announced one evening, without preamble, that she had just smoked her last cigarette. From that moment on, she'd never smoked again...until something—or, more likely, *someone*—had driven her back to the habit.

She was about to slip away from her mother's bedside, just to look out in the hall and see if Bill was around, when her mother stirred, murmuring something in her sleep.

"Mom? Mother?" Cara called softly.

Beth Dunlap's eyelids trembled and then fluttered open. She seemed to be having trouble focusing.

"It's me, Mom, Cara."

"Cara? Cara! Oh, sweet Lord."

Tears spurted from her mother's eyes, and Cara bent forward and took her in her arms, sitting on the edge of the bed. "Shh, it's okay, Mom, I'm here," she whispered, patting her mother's back reassuringly.

"You're here? How did you get here? Wh—Cara, am I sick?"

Cara sat back and let her mother see her face. "Yes, Mom, you are sick."

"Wh-what's wrong with me?" The older woman put her hand to her head. "I seem to remember...Doug fixed us drinks...and... Oh! Oh, God!" she screamed, clinging to Cara. "Fire! Cara, there's been a fire.... I..."

It took a few moments for Cara to get her mother quieted down. She didn't know if this was the right time to tell her mother the whole story, but then she decided she might as well learn from past mistakes—never again was she going to hold back or bite her tongue in favor of the truth.

She began in a quiet, even tone to tell her mother what Douglas Harvard had wrought. During the telling, Cara watched her mother's face closely, offering support when the range of emotions playing across her mother's face looked the most vulnerable. By the time Cara had brought her up to the moment, her mother's natural strength had been restored.

She was dry-eyed and sitting erect when she asked, "And where is Douglas now?"

Cara shook her head. "I don't know, Mom. I hit him pretty hard. He may have died in the fire." She held her breath, waiting for the dreaded reaction. After all, the man had been her mother's husband.

Tears slid down her mother's pale cheeks, but she kept her voice even. "That would probably be a blessing," she said quietly.

"And if he isn't, if he somehow made it out of there alive, he's going to have to face attempted-murder charges, Mom. How will you handle that?"

"On the side of justice, Cara, and without the aid of liquor or cigarettes."

They shared their first laugh in months. Cara followed that with a yawn.

"Come on, sweetie," her mother said, moving over and lifting the covers. "Cuddle up with me, and we'll have us a little nap."

Cara didn't hesitate. She was exhausted, and she was reminded of when she'd been a child and her mother had made nap time such a cozy business.

When Bill looked in a little while later, they were both sleeping.

"YOU CAN SEE why I can't leave her, can't you, Bill?" Cara said a few days later as she leaned against the car, which was across from the Dunlap house.

"She's better physically, but the trial is going to be difficult now that Harvard's sordid past has surfaced." She shivered and rubbed her arms. "Imagine, Mom married to a serial killer who'd married and murdered other widows all across the country. Just living with that knowledge is going to cause recurring nightmares."

Bill had known this moment was coming, even before Cara did, and for different reasons. That didn't make it easier.

He kept his hands shoved in his pockets and looked over the roof of the car at the mansion. From the outside, there was no evidence of damage, except for the blackened bits of window trim on the second floor. He and Cara had been staying at a local bed-and-breakfast inn while work was being done to restore the second floor of the house, and a crew had been hired to clean up the mess the fire fighters had made.

Now Beth Dunlap was about to be released from the hospital, and mother and daughter had a lot of recovery time to work through.

"Bill, I will be hearing from you now and then, won't I? I need to know you're all right."

"Sure." Bill allowed one hand the joy of touch—her hair, her downy cheek, the silken curve of her bottom lip.

"Bill?" Her eyes glistened with unshed tears and her lip quivered, but she didn't cry. "Maybe when my mom's life is back to normal, I could . . . oh, maybe visit you, wherever you are."

A glimpse of paradise in an otherwise bleak and dismal future. He made a pretense of thinking it over. "Yes, love. Maybe."

"Bill, we know Alvaretti doesn't have a clue. We know now it was Harvard who was having us followed. Don't you think it would be safe, down the road, to be together again?"

Oh, how he wished. "I'd also like to win the lottery," he said, his shoulders slumping. He put his hand back in his pocket, out of temptation's way. "What about your father's business? Aren't you going to have to take over now? At least until it can be sold, if that's what your mom decides to do?"

Cara nodded and bit her bottom lip. "Yes, I really feel like I need to help keep the company afloat, both for my father's memory, as well as for myself. But after that..."

"We'll see, love." He looked up as Lefebre came through the gates of Dunlap House.

"You're going to have Gordo to help you now, and he's going to be a witness to Wilder's attack on you and to finding the body."

Lefebre joined them. "I thought I'd say my farewell before I pick up Beth from the hospital," he told Bill.

Bill grinned, despite his heavy heart. "You've certainly become friendly with the women in the Dunlap family, pal."

"I have a way with brown-eyed damsels in distress."

Cara laughed. "You'd better not let my mother hear you call her that."

"What? Brown-eyed?"

They all laughed—weakly. It was a sad moment for all of them.

"I appreciate your hanging around here and picking up the slack, Gordo," Bill said, holding out his hand.

They shook hands. "Hey, what are friends for, Hamlin? I'm just glad you've been able to keep out of the picture so that you can have a safe start on the next leg of your journey."

They fell silent.

"I guess I'll let you two have some privacy," Lefebre said, breaking the silence. He handed Bill his card. "You can always leave a message on my machine if I'm away on a job or something."

They shook hands again and then, on mutual impulse, hugged briefly. "You've been a good friend, Gordo."

"You too, Spence," Lefebre said. Bill smiled at the sound of his real name as he watched Lefebre walk back toward the Dunlap House.

Cara felt the flood of emotions rising in her throat. When she swallowed, she swallowed salty liquid. "Here." She thrust a package at Bill, determined to keep the tears at bay.

"What's this, sandwiches for the trip?"

"It's nothing. A radio."

"A radio." Bill stripped away the wrappings from the box. It was a radio—a small portable, not much bigger than his hands.

"For in the car." She blinked, but the tears fell anyway. "So...so you won't feel lonely when you're driving."

Tears filled Bill's eyes, as well. He pulled her to him and held on desperately. "It's the most thoughtful gift I've ever received," he whispered raggedly.

Angrily, Cara swiped tears from her eyes and pushed away from him. "Yeah? Exactly how many gifts have you received in your life?"

That didn't bear thinking about. Self-pity wasn't his thing. Or at least it hadn't been before he met—the love of his life—a love he was about to lose.

He sniffed and shook his head. She handed him a tissue from what seemed like an endless supply in her jean's pocket.

"Go on, Bill," she ordered. "If we hang out here much longer, the neighbors are going to report us as vagrants."

He smiled. He loved the way her humor always got her off the hook emotionally. She was a scrapper, not at all the coward she'd considered herself.

"You're going to be a big help to your mom, Cara. And I'll be listening on my radio," he said, holding it aloft, "to follow the trial."

Their kiss was passionate, desperate, a mixture of intense love and absolute terror. Neither could tolerate the thought of how it would be just an hour from now, when the realization hit home—that they would probably never hold each other like this again.

Cara stood in the street to watch the car until it, and Bill, were gone from sight.

Minutes later, she and Lefebre were in the family Buick, headed toward the hospital to pick up her mom.

BILL READ THE SIGN along the highway. "You are leaving Greensville, Massachusetts. Have a good day."

He stopped the car and stared at the sign, the irony of it all hitting him full force. He turned and looked over his shoulder. There was the white steeple of the church the Dunlaps had built and worshiped in for a couple of centuries. About two blocks back was the high school from which Cara had graduated. She'd shown him the place with as much pride as if it were one of the best prep schools in the world. If he tilted his head, he could make out the edge of the town square, where a white gazebo was a resting place for the elderly and a play area for children.

He started to turn back, and his gaze fell on the radio. He turned it on, set it on the seat beside him and restarted the car's engine.

He was just pulling away from the shoulder when the announcement came over the radio. He slammed on the brakes and turned up the volume.

"We repeat," the announcer said, "the infamous mob leader Franco Alvaretti has been murdered in prison, where he was serving out a twenty-year sentence for tax fraud and other related federal crimes."

Numb with disbelief, his stomach spasming violently, Bill held the radio, staring at it. He turned it over. Was it a trick? Had Cara somehow— Was it a tape recorder, too?

He turned it and turned it. A sob escaped his throat. He could find no sign of a cassette door. It really was only a radio.

He looked over his shoulder again. The view was the same. There were no fireworks going off in the sky, there was no sign of a parade. All was quiet in the little town.

Nobody had any reason to celebrate this incredible news announcement.

Nobody but Cara. He came to himself then. Cara! He had to tell her the news.

He threw the car in gear and made a U-turn, headed back toward Greensville and the Dunlap house.

He was halfway there when doubt and fear took over. So what if Franco was dead? There were still his cohorts, any one of whom would gladly take up the mantle of revenge if Alvaretti had passed it along.

He pulled over to the curb and eyed the phone booth on the corner. This was not something he could spring on Cara until he was sure.

His hands shook as he counted out coins, trying to remember the phone number that for two years had been indelibly imprinted in his memory.

His heart sank when he heard a woman's voice, until he realized it was Avery's secretary.

"This is Bill Spencer," he said when he heard the lawyer's voice a couple of minutes later.

"I've been waiting to hear from you."

"It's true, then? He's dead?"

"Yes. I've just finished making the funeral arrangements, as a matter of fact."

Was that relief in Avery's voice? Bill dared to hope.

"I need to know what this means for me."

There was a meaningful pause. "What do you mean, Spence?"

"I mean, is the contract ongoing, until it's fulfilled?"

"Contract? There was no contract on you, Spence, and I would certainly have known."

"Come on, Deke, you can level with me. No way would Franco have let me just walk off into the sunset, scot-free."

Avery's chuckle was fraught with bitter irony. "Oh, no, you're right, he wouldn't have. In fact, he ordered me to have you found."

Another pause. "As you know, I was unsuccessful. I've got to hand it to you, Spence, you certainly know how to go underground."

Disbelief was his strongest emotion. He knew only too well the scope of the mob's operation—the long reach it had to all four corners of the country, the manpower and technology at its command.

"And Franco gave up? Just like that?"

He heard Avery clear his throat. "Not exactly. He ordered me to keep up the search."

"I see." He wasn't sure he did. "And you kept looking, but you had no luck, and Alvaretti accepted that."

"Er... let's just say Alvaretti got caught up in politics at the prison." Bill could have sworn he heard Avery smother a laugh just then. "In the end, it was prison politics that killed him."

"And now what, Deke?"

Another of those strange pauses. But when Avery spoke, his tone suggested mirth. "Now Alvaretti really does go underground, as it were, and you go...wherever you like."

"It's over, then?" Bill demanded, ignoring the lawyer's self-congratulatory laughter and zeroing in on the content of his statement.

"Yes, Spence. All over."

"Listen, Deke, thanks. I mean...well, so long, Deke."

He was just about to hang up when Avery said, in a conspiratorial whisper, "If we ever *bump* into each other again, Spence, I hope it will be a friendly meeting."

Before he could react, he heard a click, and then the dial tone.

Bill hung up and stared at the phone. Had he imagined the emphasis in Deke's voice when he used the word *bump?*

He left the phone booth in a daze, mulling over the implications. If Avery was using the word as a pun, as he was prone to do, was he referring to the bumper-car concession Bill had worked at the boardwalk?

Bill turned and looked back at the phone booth, a puzzled expression on his face. But that would mean Deke had known all along where he was. And hadn't reported it to Alvaretti?

He shook his head. *Deke the geek, hold out on Franco Alvaretti? Not likely. And yet...*

He cast his mind back to the time they were in Santa Cruz, trying to get a feel for the people he'd encountered there. *Any of whom could have been an agent Avery had sent out to find him.*

He shrugged. This was a mystery he'd probably never solve.

He glanced up the street and saw the church steeple. A beacon of hope, of welcome, pointing toward heaven.

He began to run.

He didn't even think about the car, but left it where it was and ran as fast as his legs would carry him.

CARA CLOSED her mother's door and turned in the direction of her own room. From downstairs she could hear Gordon Lefebre's voice rumbling, followed by the sound of Mrs. Malcom's laughter.

Cara smiled. She had to hand it to him. Malcom was a hard nut to crack, but Gordon had managed to soften her up in record time. Cara suspected that was because the housekeeper appreciated the way Gordon catered to and pampered Beth Dunlap.

Harvard. Beth Harvard.

Hard to remember that her mother had actually married the man, maybe because the fact was so unpalatable. What she wanted was for the whole nasty business to disappear, to never have happened at all.

But with the trial set for only a month away, there was no way to play that game of pretense.

She touched the balustrade as she ambled down the hall. The workers had done a fine job of cleanup and restoration in less than a week. Though it was due in part to the power of money, Cara knew that much of it could be credited to community kindness. People were willing to go that extra mile for them because the Dunlaps had always been there for the community.

She rounded the corner. This was her first time returning to her room. She had been unable to make herself look inside, as if somehow afraid Doug's body might still be lying on the floor where she'd left it that fateful night.

How he had managed to escape the fire she would never know. Perhaps it was God's way of demanding payment by forcing Harvard to live out his life in prison.

She opened the door. It was exactly as she'd left it.

Her heart lurched in her chest when she saw the ties from the library drapes on the bed. And there on the floor was the pottery bowl, the weapon with which she'd fought off Harvard, preventing him from carrying out his plan to leave her and her mother to die in the fire he'd set.

More would come out at the trial, but already they knew the essentials: that Douglas Harvard, with a string of aliases, had murdered three other women he'd married for their money; that he'd deliberately started his wife smoking again and drinking to excess so that the whole town would know of it and ask no questions when she fell asleep with a glass of gin in one hand and a lit cigarette in the other. It would have been deemed accidental arson, set by the victim herself.

Cara took the drapery ties from the bed and dropped them in the wastebasket. There'd been no fire damage on the first floor, but those drapes in the library would have to go. There were some things that just didn't bear remembering.

"Life goes on, Cara baby," she whispered. And then she burst into tears.

She fell to the bed, curled on her side and began to sob helplessly, holding the pillow against her face to stifle the sound.

Dr. Zachary had warned her of this pending depression. It was called poststress syndrome, and he'd told her it might attack at any moment, particularly after things began to return to what she considered normal.

Her mother was home, on the mend. Doug Harvard was in jail, awaiting trial, and after he'd been convicted here, he'd be extradited to Detroit to be tried for the murder of his third wife. Gordon Lefebre had proved a friend to the household and had agreed to stay with the women throughout the trial, for moral support.

Normal.

Her sobs increased, and her body shook.

What was normal when Bill was out there, God know where, alone, on the run, leaving her here to deal with a life bereft of his smile, his voice, his touch, his love?

She fumbled blindly for tissues and blew her nose. But the tears continued to flow, and her chest heaved with the effort to pull herself together.

"Self-pity," she sobbed aloud.

And why not?

Because that wasn't her thing. She was a doer, an up-ward-looking person who usually found meaning in adversity.

Her sob broke on a laugh. "As Bill would say," she said through clenched teeth, "inappropriate humor."

She sat up, swinging her legs over the side of the bed, tears still streaming from her eyes.

"I can't believe I ever thought anything about you was inappropriate, love."

Cara screamed and then flung herself across the room, into the arms of her lover.

"What are you doing back here, where did you come from, what happened? I can't believe you're here." Endless questions and endless kisses ensued until they were both laughing and crying and barely able to keep their balance in the doorway.

"I'll tell you everything, if you'll just give me a chance," Bill said, laughing and lifting her off her feet for one last kiss. Her feet touched the floor, and she took a step backward.

"I know," she exulted, staring into his face. "I know just by looking at you. Something wonderful has happened."

"Alvaretti is dead."

A silence hung between them. Cara's mouth fell open, and Bill waited, eyebrow cocked jauntily, for her reaction.

"Go on!"

He grinned.

She frowned.

"Get over yourself, Hamlin, this isn't even funny."

"It's true."

"Oh, right," she snapped. "Big goodbye scene, tears, hugs, promises. You go off into the sunset. I stay behind, try to pick up the pieces on the home front. News flash— Villain is dead. Hero and heroine reunited. All's well with the world. Fade out!''

She marched over to the bed and plunked herself down, glaring across the room at him.

Bill stuffed his hands in his pockets, leaned against the doorframe and cocked his head to the side. "Pretty good scenario, love, almost word for word the way it was." He grinned. "I always did say you wasted your talents going into business. You should be in drama, or else take up writing."

Cara stared at him. Could it be true? She squinted. He had a different look about him. What was it? That tiny line between his eyebrows was gone. But no, that wasn't it. His jaw didn't seem so tightly set. Was that it?

"You don't look haunted anymore," she said slowly, as belief crept in.

"Because I'm not." He pushed away from the door and strolled toward her. "I'm in the clear, Cara. Free, and unencumbered by debt or threat." He stopped in front of her. "And I'm all yours, if you'll have me."

They were a different kind of tears that slipped down her cheeks as Cara lifted her arms. "Forever and ever," she whispered.

And as he took her into his arms, she whispered something else.

"What? What did you say?" he asked, while his hands were already pulling her shirt from the waistband of her jeans.

"I said, as soon as we've had a proper hello, I think you should go out and buy a lottery ticket."

Take 4 bestselling love stories FREE

Plus get a FREE surprise gift!

Special Limited-time Offer

Mail to Harlequin Reader Service®

3010 Walden Avenue
P.O. Box 1867
Buffalo, N.Y. 14269-1867

YES! Please send me 4 free Harlequin Intrigue® novels and my free surprise gift. Then send me 4 brand-new novels every month. Bill me at the low price of $2.44 each plus 25¢ delivery and applicable sales tax, if any.* That's the complete price and a savings of over 10% off the cover prices—quite a bargain! I understand that accepting the books and gift places me under no obligation ever to buy any books. I can always return a shipment and cancel at any time. Even if I never buy another book from Harlequin, the 4 free books and the surprise gift are mine to keep forever.

181 BPA ANRK

Name	(PLEASE PRINT)	
Address	Apt. No.	
City	State	Zip

This offer is limited to one order per household and not valid to present Harlequin Intrigue® subscribers. *Terms and prices are subject to change without notice.
Sales tax applicable in N.Y.

UINT-295

©1990 Harlequin Enterprises Limited

HARLEQUIN®

INTRIGUE®

Into a world where danger lurks around
every corner, and there's a fine line between trust
and betrayal, comes a tall, dark and handsome man.

Intuition draws you to him...but instinct keeps you
away. Is he really one of those...

Don't miss even one of the twelve sexy but secretive
men, coming to you one per month in 1995.

In April, look for
#317 DROP DEAD GORGEOUS
by Patricia Rosemoor

**Take a walk on the wild side...with our
"DANGEROUS MEN"!**

Available wherever Harlequin books are sold.

HARLEQUIN®

INTRIGUE®

What if...

You'd agreed to marry a man you'd never met, in a town where you'd never been, while surrounded by wedding guests you'd never seen before?

And what if...

You weren't sure you could trust the man to whom you'd given your hand?

Look for "Mail Order Brides"—the upcoming two novels of romantic suspense by Cassie Miles, which are available in April and July—and only from Harlequin Intrigue!

Don't miss

> #320 MYSTERIOUS VOWS
> by Cassie Miles
> April 1995

Mail Order Brides—where mail-order marriages lead distrustful newlyweds into the mystery and romance of a lifetime!